SCREECH OWLS

FACE-OFF AT THE ALAMO

ROY MACGREGOR

Tundra Books

Published in Canada by Tundra Books, a division of Random House of Canada Limited,
One Toronto Street, Suite 300, Toronto, Ontario M5C 2V6

Published in the United States by Tundra Books of Northern New York,
P.O. Box 1030, Plattsburgh, New York 12901

Library of Congress Control Number: 2012943702

Library and Archives Canada Cataloguing in Publication

MacGregor, Roy, 1948-
Face-off at the Alamo / Roy MacGregor.

(Screech Owls)
ISBN 978-1-77049-418-3. – ISBN 978-1-77049-423-7 (EPUB)

I. Title. II. Series: MacGregor, Roy, 1948- . Screech Owls series.

PS8575.G84F33 2013 jC813'.54 C2012-904860-7

We acknowledge the financial support of the Government of Canada through the Canada Book Fund and that of the Government of Ontario through the Ontario Media Development Corporation's Ontario Book Initiative. We further acknowledge the support of the Canada Council for the Arts and the Ontario Arts Council for our publishing program.

ONTARIO ARTS COUNCIL
CONSEIL DES ARTS DE L'ONTARIO

Designed by Jennifer Lum

www.tundrabooks.com

Printed and bound in the United States of America

1 2 3 4 5 6 18 17 16 15 14 13

For Fisher and Sadie Cation,
the next generation . . .

1

"Why don't we see how many hockey sticks we can jam into that big yap of yours?"

Travis Lindsay cringed. He'd watched this scene play out far too many times on road trips with the Screech Owls. Nish – Wayne Nishikawa, Travis's sometimes-best, sometimes-worst friend on the team – would eventually push just a bit too far, until either Sarah or Sam had heard quite enough of the ridiculous chubby defenseman and his big mouth and one of them would turn on him.

This time it was Sam: Samantha Bennett, the fiery, red-haired, peewee star who was every bit a match for Nish on the ice and, usually, more than a match off it.

"Or why don't we use your mouth at practice and see how many pucks we can dump into it?"

There were times when Travis thought that his job as team captain was to make sure all the Screech Owls got along. But there were also times, he knew, when his job was to drag his pal Nish back down to earth.

The peewee hockey team from little Tamarack in Canada had been filling in time between flights – a short layover in Chicago before heading on to San Antonio, Texas – when Nish went into one of his all-too-familiar sugar attacks. He was flying so high, Sarah suggested he wouldn't even need a seat on the plane.

In a way, it had partly been Data's fault. Data – real name Larry Ulmar, though no one had called him that since kindergarten – was the team's ultimate geek, a web surfer supreme who not only knew how to fix computers but seemed to have a hard drive installed between his ears. Ever since

Data's accident – struck by a drunk driver and unable to walk or skate since – Data had been serving as the team's assistant coach and full time wireless guru. He helped run the team's power play, but he also fixed the cell phones, downloaded the apps, programmed the laptops and various tablets and music players as well as running a Screech Owls website that would have been the envy of any club in the National Hockey League.

Data had been using the Internet to find out all he could about their destination: San Antonio, Texas, home of the San Antonio Peewee Invitational hockey tournament. It wasn't long before he came across a link that took him to San Antonio's Ripley's Believe It or Not – just across the street from the Alamo, the famous fort where Davy Crockett had fought and died, and where many believe the American love of freedom was born. Data got so excited about the Ripley's exhibition he forgot all about the Alamo. He called Travis and the rest of the Owls over, and almost instantly he'd been bumped off his own tablet and Nish was drooling over the screen like a big dog over a barbecued steak.

"They got a wax museum there, too!" the big defenseman shouted, his face squeezing into that red-tomato look Travis had come to recognize as a warning light. Something was coming. Something totally wacko. Something totally Nish.

In an instant, Nish's thick fingers were flicking through shots of the famous characters in the waxworks and he was shouting out their names as if only he was capable of recognizing the celebrities.

"Michael Jackson!

"Marilyn Monroe!

"The President!

"Elvis!"

And that, of course, was what really got him going. If his great hero, Elvis Presley, could be a wax figure in San Antonio, Nish figured he should be, too.

"By the time I get named tournament MVP," Nish loudly boasted, "they'll be measuring me up for *my* wax statue!"

Travis could see Sam shaking her head in disgust. But Nish wasn't finished.

"It's *perfect!*" he screeched. "I'll be in Ripley's

Believe It or Not for my amazing play in this tournament. And I'll be a wax celebrity with my pal Elvis. San Antonio is *my* kind of town!"

Nish soon had all the Owls going through the Ripley's website. They snorted at the man with the world's largest nose – "*You'd need a backhoe to pick that monster!*" shouted Andy Higgins – and they stared in amazement at the man with the world's biggest eyes. They argued over whether some of the claims were real – the two-headed calf, the half man, the bearded lady – and they squirmed uncomfortably when they looked at the Lizard Man, with his green skin and surgically split tongue.

When they saw photographs of the man from India who had let the fingernails of one hand grow to more than twenty feet long, Sam pretended to put her fingers – nails bitten to the quick – down her throat to make herself throw up. When they saw the man who was able to lift more than a hundred pounds – just about the weight of the average Screech Owl – using only his *ears*, several of the Owls covered the sides of their heads as if they were being pulled up into a tree by nothing but their earlobes.

It didn't take long for Nish to see an opening for himself – an opening as big as his troublesome mouth.

"Here's a world record I can get!" he announced.

The team crowded around Data's little computer and stared at a page about Jim Purol, "the World's Biggest Mouth."

"Perfect!" sneered Sam.

"The record's already yours," teased Sarah.

The story about Purol was bizarre. He had set twenty-three world records, more than anyone else. He had set his historic twenty-third record at the Rose Bowl football stadium when he sat in 39,250 seats in two days. But that wasn't what interested Nish, who had never been known to sit still long enough to keep count.

"151 straws!" Nish shouted. "151? I can beat that, *easy*!"

Travis had no idea what Nish was yapping about. He pushed his way through the gathering to see for himself. There was a YouTube video of Jim Purol stuffing more drinking straws into his mouth than you'd find at your local McDonald's.

"I can do it!" Nish said. "Help me collect some straws!"

And so began the Great Straw Hunt at Chicago's O'Hare Airport. Under Nish's direction, the Owls set off from the loading gate toward the food court area, where each one stepped up to the various fast-food outlets – MCD's, Wendy's, DQ, a half-dozen others – to pretend they'd neglected to pick up a straw with their meal and took as many as three or four at a time.

They made their way back to the gate and huddled in a corner well away from Muck Munro, the team's coach, and Mr. Dillinger, the manager, who were drinking coffee and playing a game of hearts to pass the time until they boarded the plane to San Antonio.

As each of the Owls unwrapped the straws he or she had picked up and passed them on to Fahd Noorizadeh, the team's little defenseman, Nish lay flat on his back on a row of seats, mouth open wide as a garbage can. One by one, Fahd placed the straws into Nish's big mouth while the other Owls kept count.

"Forty!" Fahd announced triumphantly after several minutes.

"*Uhhmmmm!*" Nish shouted, sounding as if his mouth had been duct-taped over.

"Fifty!"

"Fifty-five!"

"Fifty-six!"

"Seven!"

"Eight!"

"*Uhhhhmmmmmmmmmm!*" Nish shouted, his eyes bulging.

"*Fifty-NINE!*" Fahd called out, shaking his head. "That's it, folks, the World's Biggest Mouth is full up!"

"Wow," said Sam with great sarcasm, "only ninety-three short! The world record is just about yours, Big Mouth!"

Nish sputtered and spat, the straws flying out of his mouth and onto the seats and floor all around the Owls.

"*No fair!*" he shouted when he'd spat the last one out. "These straws are fatter than what that guy used."

"The only thing fat around here is you," said Sam. "As in, *fat chance!*"

Nish glared at her, his eyes mere slits in his beet-red face.

Travis couldn't help himself. He started to giggle.

2

It had been a long off-season. Muck's rules for the Screech Owls were unbreakable. He alone among the coaches in the Tamarack area would have nothing to do with summer hockey. He said summer was for *families*, not just kids. The Screech Owls should try other sports in the summer, he told them. He had this theory that all games feed into each other and help each other. Play soccer, he would say, and see how it's possible to attack by first turning back. Play lacrosse, he would say, and find out for yourself what magic Wayne Gretzky discovered when he went behind the net to make his plays. Play baseball, and learn the art of bunting – it's not that far from tipping shots from the point in hockey.

Travis had spent the early part of his summer playing soccer and lacrosse, and then passed the entire month of August at his grandparents' cottage in the north. He went wakeboarding almost every day and mastered both the "360" and the full flip – how, he wondered to himself, would Muck apply those two skills to hockey? – and he had fished and canoed and swam and eaten more s'mores and burnt marshmallows around the campfire than he could count. He figured he must have finally put some weight on his small frame and was disappointed to return home to Tamarack, hop on his mother's bathroom scale, and discover he was exactly the same 103 pounds he had been when the family left for the cottage. He felt stronger, though, and was already looking forward to the new season with the Owls.

It seemed forever since he had skated. At one point, he went down into the basement and dressed himself in his full hockey gear. It felt so strange, as he dragged his equipment out of the storage bin, that he wondered if he could even recall how to dress, let alone play.

And yet the moment Travis placed that first pad over his right shin, it all came flooding back. He had once read that you never forget, no matter how old you are, how to ride a bicycle or how to swim, and he knew it was the same for getting dressed for hockey. Over the years, he had developed a ritual. First right shin pad, then left. Then jock and garter belt pulled up over the shin pads. Socks on next – first right, then left – then attach the tops to the Velcro strips on the garter. Then hockey pants, but never done up right away: fly tie left open, shoulder straps left hanging.

It was such a strange routine to go through. Travis felt like he was *inhaling* his hockey equipment, sucking in familiar smells that his mother could never wash out completely at the end of the season. He pulled on his shoulder pads and breathed deeply. Then his elbow pads, first right elbow, then left. He put on his neck guard, convinced his neck was thicker – a sure sign he would be a stronger player this year. He had always been quick, always sneaky, always able to read the play and see the ice as well as anyone else on the team – Sarah Cuthbertson excepted – but he desperately wished he could be stronger in the corners, tougher on face-offs, and have a harder shot. If he could only fire the puck like Dmitri Yakushev – Dmitri of the patented backhander that sent the opposing goaltender's water bottle flying through the air and into the glass back of the net every time – then he would be the complete player: Travis Lindsay, NHL-bound.

Next, he tried on his skates. They had their own particular smell – a touch of plastic, a hint of steel – but they felt like cement blocks. Feet that had gone bare most of the summer suddenly were crammed in tight. Had they grown? In a way, he hoped not – these Eastons were the best skates he had ever worn – in another way, he couldn't help but hope he had got a bit bigger.

He tied them tight. The skates felt impossibly awkward. They always did at the start of a new season. Travis had a theory that your *real* hockey season arrived the moment you ceased to think about skating and it just happened, with the skates becoming natural extensions of your own skin and bone. The moment you no longer *thought* about playing, you really *were* playing. For Travis, this feeling came about a month into the season, a few weeks after the first tryouts and a week or two after the first league game. From then on, he was a *player*.

He pulled his Screech Owls practice jersey over his head and paused, as always, to kiss the crest just as it passed by his mouth. He wouldn't feel right if he didn't do this each time he dressed. He knew how silly it might appear to anyone who saw, but no one ever saw, and the only person he had ever told was Sarah, who admitted to the same silly ritual.

Next came the helmet – the inside filled with smells as familiar as the rink itself. He could almost see the Zamboni sliding slightly on the final turn of a fresh flood.

He put on his gloves, spat on them both, as they felt dry and cumbersome. He picked up his stick – his first full graphite, still like new, though he had used it since he got it last Christmas from his grandparents – and leaned over as if he had finally reached the NHL and was posing for his rookie hockey card.

He felt awkward. He felt encased and enclosed after a summer of total freedom. How, in a single week, could he possibly have gone from a bathing suit to this suit of armor? He felt he wouldn't be able to skate. The stick felt all wrong in his hands, the gloves dry and stubborn as he tried to grip the stick.

Travis laughed. He knew this moment well. He always tried his hockey equipment on at the end of summer. It always felt completely wrong. And it always felt completely right the instant he took his first step out on the ice, his skates digging in on that first corner of freshly flooded ice and his ankle flicking to send a spray of still-unfrozen water.

He could hardly wait to get going.

Tryouts had gone as expected. Muck and Mr. Dillinger had their team – the same players as last season. They liked it just the way it was and weren't keen on change. Muck had so many theories, Travis had trouble remembering some of them, but one he would never forget was Muck's belief that a good *team* beat good players. Several times he had seen Muck and Mr. Dillinger look impressed by a new player who came out and showed great skill on the ice, only to cut the player after a couple of practices. Be selfish with the puck and you wouldn't become an Owl. Take stupid penalties and you wouldn't be an Owl. Be a "hot dog" – which sounded like a swear word the way Muck said it – and you would never, ever join the Owls.

None of this, of course, explained how Nish kept his position on Muck Munro's Screech Owls. Nothing Travis could think of explained Wayne Nishikawa. All Travis knew for certain was that, for all the trouble that Nish caused, when the crunch came in an important game, the big defenseman with the beet-red face and the hockey puck for a brain would be there. And could be counted on.

Camp ended and the Owls played a couple of exhibition games against a good peewee team from Buffalo – the junior Sabres – before beginning their season. It was just before Thanksgiving that Mr. Dillinger sent the note out to the Screech Owls' parents that soon had the team talking about nothing else.

The Owls had been invited to the San Antonio Peewee Invitational – and Mr. Dillinger and Muck were both recommending that the team should go. Muck pitched the trip as "educational." The tournament had been set up to include guided tours of the Alamo, and the championship team was to get the opportunity to spend the night camped out in the world's most famous fort.

Muck, a history buff, couldn't resist. The Screech Owls' coach would be in heaven in San Antonio.

But he had no idea how close he would come to going to heaven for good.

3

The Screech Owls landed at San Antonio International Airport on the Thursday morning leading into the Thanksgiving holiday. The airports had been packed – Thanksgiving being the biggest travel weekend in the American year – and the Owls were happy to get out onto the open road again for the bus ride into the city.

If the Owls' world was a coin, it felt as if someone had flipped it. They had left in sleet – their flight out was delayed while ground crew de-iced the wings – and landed in sun so strong they could have fried eggs on the wings of the big US Airways jet that brought them to a halt at the airport terminal. They had left a world of high hills, deep bush, and freshwater lakes and landed in virtual desert, the ground brown and dusty, the hills low and rolling, the sky seeming to stretch on forever without meeting the horizon. Trees were the exception here, whereas back in Tamarack they were so much the rule that the town had been named after one.

The community was also a reversal. Tamarack was tiny; San Antonio was huge, its population nearly one and a half million. If there was a similarity between the two places, it was a stretch: Tamarack had a gentle river splitting the town in half; San Antonio had River Walk, a series of shallow canals that turned and twisted through a maze of shops and restaurants in the city's downtown. Tamarack's river had snowmobiles moving along it in winter, canoes and speedboats in summer when the tourist season began. San Antonio's canals had small water taxis. They moved through a city that seemed, Travis thought, to be locked in an eternal tourist season.

Then there was the hockey rink. Travis took one look inside the Ice Center at Northwoods – home of the American Hockey League's Rampage – and felt like he had just stepped through a time machine right back into Tamarack's Memorial Arena.

Sure, the San Antonio rink was much newer and far larger, but there was the same smell of Dustbane cleaner, even the same soft whisking sound of one of the arena staff slowly pushing a broom across the cement floor of the lobby. There were the same bright lights slowly popping on, one by one, then in bunches, as the arena was lit up before the Owls' first skate. There was the sound of skates being sharpened coming from a back room – a grating, singing, hot sound that, only to the ear of a hockey player, is pure music. And then there was the ice: glistening, hard, smooth, an off-white color bordered by the startling bright blues and reds of the painted lines and face-off circles.

Travis was home.

So, too, was Nish.

If Travis thought his best friend had come

down from his sugar attack since the flight from Chicago, he was wrong. If anything, Nish was even more wound up. And he was already causing trouble.

Travis had been driven to the rink by his billets, Mr. and Mrs. Finebester, who had also taken in Little Simon Milliken, Dmitri, and Derek Dillinger. The four Owls arrived after the rest of the team, and for once Travis was glad to be late.

Nish had somehow arrived first. He had, as might be expected, immediately set to work with his ridiculous pranks. First he had loaded up a garbage pail with water and carefully balanced it on the dressing-room door so that the next person to shove open the door dumped the pail on his head.

That would be Jesse Highboy, sitting soaked to the skin and looking miserable in a locker in the far corner of the room.

Nish had also taken advantage of Mr. Dillinger's hard work with the equipment. Mr. D had neatly laid out the players' equipment in their stalls, each with a name tag and number filled out by the Owls' manager with a thick Sharpie pen. He had placed the shin pads, carefully turned right side up, above each locker. Nish had taken note and filled several of the pads with cups of water, knowing that none of the Owls was tall enough to see and would simply reach up and yank the pads down.

That would be Gordie Griffith and Fahd, each sitting in another corner with soaking wet faces and hair.

Travis shook his head and refused to give the giggling, red-faced Nish the attention that he craved. He tried to concentrate on the music pounding out from Data's fancy sound system, but not even his favorite hockey tune – Queen's "We Are the Champions" – could distract Travis as much as he wished from the locker next to him.

Nish had his equipment bag open, and it seemed to be filled with rotting dead animals. How, Travis wondered, could such a stink survive all summer long? Did Nish not get his equipment washed like everyone else? Did he not notice? Or did he just not care?

Travis was late because Mr. Finebester had been held up in traffic on his way home. Mr. Finebester had hurried to get his four guests to the rink, but by the time they arrived, the rest of the Owls were already well into their dressing. The three girls – Sam, Sarah, and goaltender Jenny Staples – were already in full equipment and doing stretches outside the room they had been assigned.

Travis hurried, but he stuck to his ritual: right, left, right, left. . . . He kissed his practice jersey as he pulled it on and bent over to hurry up with his skates. He grabbed the right laces first, carefully looping the long ends through the fingers of each hand, and pulled up hard.

Snap!

The laces broke. And so, too, did Nish. He burst like a balloon that has been blown up too tightly, air and spit spraying the room as well as poor Travis. Nish, fully dressed himself, leaped to his feet and with great drama tapped his little captain on the shin pads.

"Let's go, Trav! You're running late!"

Travis looked up, his face burning red. He could see his teammates laughing at him, though some didn't dare to look his way.

He had just been caught in hockey's dumbest prank – the half-cut skate laces. He tried his left skate, grabbing the laces and pulling hard. *Snap!*

Caught twice.

Travis groaned. He would now have to unlace both skates and thread in new ones – carefully crossing them in the pattern Sarah had taught him – and he wouldn't be out in time for Muck's whistle.

Muck would not be amused.

The rest of the team hurried out and onto the ice while Travis furiously sought to replace his laces and catch up. He finished, pulled on his helmet and his gloves, jumped up, and yanked his stick from the stick rack.

It felt different.

But nothing really felt right to Travis. He still didn't have the feeling that his skates were part of his own body. He still hadn't reached that soaring moment in the season when it was no longer necessary to think about what he was doing on the ice. Instead, he lumbered around the rink a couple of times, trying to ignore Muck's hard stare and the slow shake of his head. He did his quick stretches and then lined up for a few practice shots at Jenny Staples and Jeremy Weathers in goal.

Travis was next after Lars Johanssen, the nifty little defenseman who had moved from Sweden to Tamarack and who was so slick with the puck. Lars picked up Muck's pass from the corner, raced in, hit the brakes just as Jeremy guessed he was about to go around him, and waited while Jeremy slid out past him. Lars was all alone with the puck on his stick and a completely empty net. The rest of the Owls pounded their sticks on the ice in admiration as Lars, as gently as if he were pushing an egg, deposited the puck in the net.

Now it was Travis's turn. The puck bounced awkwardly off his stick and away. He had to skate back to pick it up.

The puck felt all wrong. His stick seemed to weigh a ton. He felt weak. He knew what he wanted to do, what he *always* wanted to do: put the puck off the crossbar. He never cared during practice or warm-up whether or not he scored. It was far more important to hit the crossbar.

He skated in, feeling like he was using someone else's legs. He set himself to shoot, feeling like someone else's arms were holding his stick. He shot, and the stick was like a lead pipe in his hands.

The puck never even left the ice.

Travis cut back. He could hear pounding. Sticks on the ice. He looked over his shoulder. All his teammates were saluting him as if he had just scored the greatest double-fake, between-the-legs goal in hockey history.

Sarah, giggling, skated over and took Travis's stick out of his hand. She glided to the penalty box and carefully used the blade of her skate to pop off the rubber plug at the top of Travis's stick before she returned it to him.

Someone had filled it with water.

He didn't need to ask who. Travis looked for Nish and saw him skating loops and circles by the far boards. Nish, acting as if nothing whatsoever had happened, was wearing his best choirboy face.

Travis hated that look.

4

Dmitri was the first to say out loud what every one of the Owls was thinking.

"Is it ever *small*!"

The Screech Owls had come downtown from their various billets in the surrounding San Antonio suburbs. Travis, Simon, Dmitri, and Derek were all staying with the Finebesters in Hill Country Village, out by the airport. Nish and Fahd were in a nearby development called Hollywood Park – "Naturally," Nish boasted, "they put me up in

Hollywood" – and various Owls were staying with families in different parts of the city itself, all within short driving distance of the downtown core and the famous River Walk.

They had parked at the Rivercenter Mall and first toured through River Walk. Travis wondered what Tamarack would look like with a similar development. He could not imagine two floors of shops built along the banks of the river back home. Or seeing the alders and Scotch pines all along its banks replaced by the huge planters filled with shrubs and flowers that gave River Walk a slightly sickly sweet smell. Instead of the canoes and speedboats back home and the kids diving off the Tamarack bridge after the boats had passed under it, they would have to move about in small gondolas poled from end to end and around the sweeping corners of the shopping area. It just wouldn't work back in Tamarack.

Travis and Derek ran onto the first bridge across the canal and tried to see down into the water to check for fish, but either the water was too dark or there were none. There were few pleasures

Travis enjoyed more than lying on the side of the Tamarack bridge after a good swim and gazing down into the clear water at the smallmouth bass that slipped in and out of the shadows along the wooden footings of the bridge. Sometimes he saw a huge snapping turtle just lying in the water, lazily looking up at the divers lounging about on the side of the bridge, who refused to drop again until the turtle had moved on. There was no such life apparent in the canals that cut through San Antonio, but you would never say River Walk was not lively. There were shoppers and tourists everywhere, and several of the restaurants had live entertainment, including a very loud mariachi band playing on the patio outside a Mexican restaurant.

The team would eat later. First Muck wanted them to see what San Antonio is most famous for. He wanted them not only to see it but to hear about it and think about it.

Travis had tried to imagine the Alamo. He knew it was a fort. He had seen an old Disney movie where John Wayne played the hero Davy Crockett, and it seemed to him the fort was huge – sort of a wooden castle in the middle of the desert. The last thing in the world he expected when they arrived at the Alamo was a tiny little earthen wall in the heart of the downtown core. It looked like a child's fort, a play fort – it couldn't possibly be real.

But all Travis had to do was watch Muck to know that this place was important. As he entered the Alamo, Muck removed his Owls baseball cap. He looked up toward the Stars and Stripes and the flag of Texas, and it seemed to Travis as if the Screech Owls' coach were walking into a church.

"This is *it*?" hissed Nish.

The big defenseman didn't even bother to hide his disappointment. He had almost broken away from the pack to run to Ripley's Believe It or Not across the street, but he hadn't dared. He knew how much this visit to the Alamo meant to Muck.

"It's *miniature*," said Sarah, speaking far more in awe than insult.

Muck had arranged for a special tour. The Owls were met by a uniformed ranger – Bill Norton of the U.S. National Park Service, according to the badge on his shirt – who took them off to a presentation room and told them the story of the Battle of the Alamo using old photographs, artwork, and a video presentation.

Travis was fascinated to learn that one of the commanders of the fort had been William Travis – sort of a namesake – and that the other commander had been Jim Bowie. Several of the Owls had heard of the famous Bowie knife, and the ranger said that Jim Bowie was its inventor.

Texas was not yet a state in 1836, the ranger told them, and Mexico and the "Texians" – as the mostly American settlers in Texas were called – were at war to see who would control the land. The Texians were terribly outnumbered, with maybe a hundred or so to defend the little fort against the 1,500 Mexican soldiers who were marching on them. The Alamo wasn't even a real fort, the ranger said, but a sort of rough barricade to protect the settlers against Native raids on their horses and supplies. It could not possibly survive attack by a well-equipped army. There were barracks, a chapel, a well, storage houses, and walls, but the walls were so low they didn't even have portals for the defenders to fire from.

The ranger told them how William Travis had begged for reinforcements, but only about a hundred showed up, including Davy Crockett, the famous "King of the Wild Frontier" from Tennessee. The moment Ranger Norton mentioned Crockett and his famous rifle, Ol' Betsy, Mr. Dillinger shocked the group by breaking into song.

"*Born on a mountain top in Tennessee,*" Mr. Dillinger sang in a high, creaky voice, "*greenest state in the Land of the Free.*"

But then Muck, of all people, joined in even louder, until in a moment the three grown men – Mr. Dillinger, Muck, and the ranger – were all singing and laughing together.

"What was *that*?" Fahd asked.

"The Davy Crockett song," the ranger explained. "Don't you kids know it?"

"No."

"Well, then, you're missing an important part of your history. Your two coaches sure know it."

"My favorite song when I was a kid," Mr. Dillinger said. "We used to live for the TV show."

"They had TV back *then*?" Nish asked, as if Mr. Dillinger had been born long before the dinosaurs. Mr. Dillinger shot him daggers.

"There are a hundred stories about Davy Crockett," Ranger Norton told them. "Some of them are true, some are tall tales. Supposedly he killed a bear that was threatening the Crockett family when he was only three years old. And according to legend, he used Old Betsy, his rifle, to kill some 125 bears in his lifetime."

"Do *you* believe it?" asked Fahd, who always asked the most direct questions.

"Well, I don't know otherwise," the ranger said. "Some say Davy went down at the Alamo swinging Ol' Betsy like a club, the fighting so fierce he had no time to reload. Some say he had given it to his son before he ever even came to Texas. We just don't know. But people certainly believe that's the way he died."

"What happened to the rifle?" asked Nish.

"No idea," the ranger said. "Burned, likely, with everything else at the end of the battle."

Ranger Norton got back to his talk. When the Mexican army arrived at the fort, a siege began that lasted for thirteen days, but the taking of the fort took less than an hour. The Mexicans simply overwhelmed the defenders. They killed some 250 Americans, though it was estimated that the determined defenders of the fort killed or wounded as many as six hundred Mexican fighters. No mercy was shown to the defenders, who, if they hadn't been killed in combat, were executed on the spot. It was said that Davy Crockett was found surrounded by more than a dozen Mexican soldiers he had killed before he died, supposedly dispatching most of them by using his faithful rifle as a club. The sole survivors were a handful of women and children who had hidden in the chapel during the fighting.

"Why does the Alamo matter?" the ranger asked. None of the Owls offered an opinion, so the ranger answered his own question. "From that moment on," he said, "the Alamo stood as an inspiration for freedom and for fighting for what you believe in."

He clicked a handheld control, and a portrait of William Travis appeared on the screen. Travis was surprised to learn how young his almost-namesake was, only twenty-six. The famous Travis of the Alamo had light brown, slightly curling hair, much like Travis Lindsay, and they both had sharp, straight noses.

"Looks like Travis's older brother!" giggled Sam.

Travis blushed deeply, but inside he was delighted. William Travis was a great hero. Travis Lindsay only had heroic dreams.

Ranger Norton told them about the letter William Travis had written at the beginning of the siege. He addressed it "To the People of Texas & All Americans in the World," and in it he penned the words for which he would forever be remembered: "I shall *never* surrender or retreat."

A true soldier fights on, no matter the odds, William Travis argued in his letter. There can be no giving up. A true soldier, he wrote, can choose only "victory or death."

Travis Lindsay sneaked a quick glance around the room. His teammates were paying rapt attention – even Nish, whom one teacher had said could serve as the poster boy for attention deficit.

In a far corner of the room, standing slightly apart from the rest of the team, Travis noticed Muck. The coach was watching so intently it seemed to Travis that Muck's eyes were flashing with light. Or perhaps they were glistening; it was hard to tell.

The friendly ranger told them how, when William Travis realized that a full attack would come at any moment and they did not stand a chance, he had taken his sword – the ranger took them outside and showed them the exact spot where this had taken place – and drawn a line in the sand. William Travis then asked all those who were willing to die for their cause to cross over the line, and he said that any who wished to flee before the Mexicans launched their assault were free to do so.

Every man in the Alamo crossed over the line.

Even Jim Bowie, too ill to stand, crossed over, lying in a cot carried by his men. Bowie was said to have fought to the bitter end even while lying in his bed, a pistol in one hand, his famous knife in the other.

The ranger then asked the Owls to follow him into the little chapel. Inside, they gathered around a large, ornate box.

"When the battle was over," the ranger said, "the Mexican soldiers gathered up the bodies of the Alamo defenders, placed them in a huge pile, and set fire to them. This crypt," he said solemnly, "holds the ashes of those who died here fighting for what they believed in."

He took them on a walk through the large courtyard, past the fort's well, and over to the huge white memorial built where the bodies had been piled and then burned. Travis read the plaque on the front: "They chose never to surrender or retreat; these brave hearts with flag still proudly waving perished in the flames of immortality that their high sacrifice might lead to the founding of this Texas."

Ranger Norton told them that no one had ever forgotten what happened here, when these brave people stood up against impossible odds and refused to give in. More than a hundred years later, this small fort in Texas was still an inspiration. In World War II, American soldiers heading into battle would often shout out, "Remember the Alamo!"

"Remember the Alamo," a voice said very quietly from the back of the little room.

Travis turned just enough to see where the voice had come from. It was Muck, and there was no longer any question whether his eyes were glistening or merely reflecting the light.

5

A small crowd was gathered around the stick rack when Travis and his fellow billets – Derek, Dmitri, and Simon – arrived for the first match of the San Antonio Peewee Invitational hockey tournament.

Travis ducked in under the arm of big Gordie Griffith and tried to see what had attracted all the attention. It seemed, at first, like nothing. The Screech Owls' game sticks were all laid out in order, just as Mr. Dillinger always put them. The players had already taped their blades to their own specifications and done whatever else they wished to the sticks. Fahd, for example, liked a knob of red tape at the top of his. Dmitri liked to wind tape up the shaft of his stick in the fashion of a barber's pole, convinced that he had a better grip when there was a bit of tape over the slippery shaft. Each stick, however, had the same lettering on the top of the shaft Mr. Dillinger carefully printed each player's name and number with a permanent pen so he could keep the sticks in order.

Travis ran his eyes along the line: Jeremy's goal sticks with their big No. 1 to start the rack, then Sam Bennett's No. 4, Data's No. 6 (kept on the rack out of respect, even though Data was no longer able to play since the accident), Travis's No. 7, and so on. And then, suddenly, Travis saw that one was different.

On the four sticks belonging to No. 44, the name "Nish" was covered over with white tape. A brand-new name had been written on top: Ol' Betsy.

"What's with that?" Travis asked.

Gordie giggled. "Nish has decided he's Davy Crockett, I guess."

Shaking his head, Travis squirreled his way back out of the crowd staring at the stick. He looked around for Nish. He found him sitting in his stall, bent over his skates so his face was out of sight. As Travis dropped his bag in front of the stall beside his friend, Nish looked up, his beet-red face beaming. But there was something else.

What was that black hole in Nish's face? He looked like he'd been shot with one of the Alamo's cannonballs and it had stuck fast between his chubby cheeks.

Nish sort of exploded – at least he *popped*, loudly – and the black object flew from his mouth and skipped hard across the dressing-room floor.

It was a puck! Nish had been sitting there with a puck in his mouth.

"*I'm practicing!*" he gasped. "*Just practicing . . .*"

"Practicing *what*?" Travis asked.

"The straws record, idiot!" Nish barked. "I'm trying to stretch out my mouth so I can get the record."

"With a puck?"

"It's perfect! Stretches my mouth just right. I'm trying to sit with a puck in my mouth for an hour a day. I think it's working."

With this, Nish opened his mouth as wide as possible in Travis's direction. Travis just shook his head and reached up for his shin pads, remembering to step slightly aside in case Nish had filled them with water.

Better to change the subject, Travis thought. "Your stick," he said. "What's with the Ol' Betsy bit? You've got to be kidding."

But Nish was suddenly serious. "Davy Crockett's in the wax museum," he hissed. "And you can buy his cap at the souvenir shop. I think it looks good, don't you?"

He reached up in his stall behind his helmet and brought down a Davy Crockett coonskin cap, which he pulled on over his face. It looked like some roadkill was sitting on his shoulders.

"Cool, eh?"

"I think you look ridiculous."

"Whatever," Nish said. "But I'm the closest

this team has to a Davy Crockett, so I'm going to wear it before every game."

"How can you say that?" Travis asked. "Davy Crockett died fighting in a war – you're a peewee hockey player!"

Nish looked up, his eyes narrowing with contempt for whatever it was Travis was trying to say.

"Hockey is war," Nish said with great dignity. "And I'm going to be the hero of this tournament."

But Nish had no idea how very true that would turn out to be.

6

Travis was starting to feel like his old self. He had checked his sticks to make sure there was no joking going on today – this, after all, was a game, not a practice – and he had dressed in perfect order, even lightly planting that kiss over the *C* as he pulled his beloved Screech Owls jersey over his head.

Even better, he had cranked his very first warm-up shot off the crossbar, causing Jeremy to roar in triumph from behind his new goal mask with the Transformer-like Screech Owl painted on. Jeremy knew, as every Owl did, that if Travis hit the bar on his first shot, it meant a good game for their captain.

And they would need him to put in a good game. Muck wasn't a speech maker, but he had something to say today. They'd be meeting the Kansas City Cheetahs, a team that had come down to San Antonio on their own bus – a spectacular vehicle with a huge pouncing yellow cheetah painted on each side and the team name front and back. But just because the Cheetahs came from a place where hockey was a rarity, Muck didn't want the Owls to take this first match lightly.

"Look," he told them, "I hear this team is going into this tournament as the favorite."

"They haven't seen *us*!" shot Sam.

Muck sent her a withering look that shut her up. He might not make many speeches, but he expected them to listen to what he did have to say.

"I played against their coach in junior, and also with him. We became pretty good friends in the short time we spent on the same team. His name's Butch Ruby. He had a minor-league career and ended up in Kansas City playing for the Red Wings in the old Central Hockey League. That was tough hockey, and Butch was one of the toughest. It was good hockey, too. The Red Wings were the farm team of the Detroit Red Wings – sent some good players on to the NHL. But not Butch. All he could do was fight. But he was awfully good at that.

"So it will be a tough and a dirty team. That's why I want you to keep your tempers in line – *you hear me, Nishikawa?* – and no retaliation. If we beat them, we do it on skill and teamwork. You got that?"

"*Got it!*" shouted Sarah, who was rocking back and forth hard in her stall. Travis smiled to himself. Sarah was already into the game.

"It's going to be rough," Muck said. "But we've got speed and skill going for us, so long as we keep our heads on right – *you got that, Nishikawa?*"

Travis didn't need to look to his side to know

that Nish was nodding up and down hard. He, too, was ready. It was going to be a great game.

Travis could never decide whether he preferred full contact or no hitting. Different leagues had different rules at the peewee level, meaning different tournaments sometimes had different rules in play. Mr. Dillinger had explained that this tournament would allow what they were calling "coincidental contact" – in other words, hits that couldn't be avoided, say, when two players went after the puck in the corners or when a forward tried to squeeze past a defenseman along the boards. But no direct, deliberate hits.

"That's how the women play the Olympics," noted Sarah.

"I don't wanna play *girls'* rules!" whined Nish, expecting his teammates to laugh along with him. But no one did. How could they, when Sarah was the team's best player?

However, "coincidental contact" turned out to be a joke. The officials were confused about what was allowed, and the Cheetahs had come to the game as if prepared to invade an alien planet. If they'd had laser guns instead of hockey sticks in their hands, Travis was convinced they'd happily use them.

He was hit hard right off the opening face-off. Sarah had used her amazing ability to cuff a dropping puck out of the air before it even touched the ice, and Travis, anticipating her move, had jumped on the play hoping to scoot around the winger opposite and pick up the puck on the other side.

He felt like he'd been hit by a truck. The big winger opposite him had stepped as hard as he could with his shoulder into Travis's chest, sending him sprawling into the boards.

Travis could hear Mr. Dillinger screaming at the referee. Muck never screamed at anyone, but sometimes Mr. Dillinger did. There was no whistle.

Travis picked himself up, noting that he was now soaked along one leg. In this warm weather, the ice hadn't even had time to freeze. He knew to be careful with passes on ice like this; they could sometimes stick fast, as if they'd run into a spot of glue.

But wet ice could also work to your advantage. Time and time again, he had seen defensemen try a little "slip" play, leaving the puck and letting it slide past a check as the defenseman stepped out of the way. If you knew how to "read" a checking player's skates, it could work beautifully, the puck slipping between the player's skates as he blew helplessly past. But not on wet ice.

Travis noted that the Kansas defenseman had moved up on the puck that Sarah had flicked forward off the face-off. Travis charged him hard, making sure his skates were well apart in the hope that he could sucker the defender into trying to slip the puck past.

It worked. The defenseman faked a pass and then lightly touched the puck forward, sidestepping quickly to move around Travis. Travis used his left skate to drag the blade along the ice, perfectly catching the puck stalled in the wet ice and kicking it up onto his own stick blade. The defenseman had conveniently stepped aside, thinking Travis would fly by, and Travis found himself open and clear.

He looked back. Sarah was driving hard to the net. Behind Sarah was Nish, charging hard, too.

Travis waited until Sarah had taken the other Kansas defender along with her to the side of the net, then hit her with a pass.

The Cheetahs' goaltender, reading the play, slid to that side to block her shot. The one remaining defensive player put his stick into Sarah's back, hitting hard.

But Sarah had no intention of shooting. She had seen – or perhaps heard – how strongly Nish was coming up the ice, and she had tapped the puck back between her skates, leaving it on the ice directly in front of the Cheetahs' open net.

Nish simply guided the puck in.

Owls 1, Cheetahs 0 – and the game wasn't fifteen seconds old.

As Nish curled back, stick high in the air, he was hit by the same vicious shoulder that had slammed Travis. This time, however, the referee's whistle screamed.

Nish went down hard, spinning along the ice as he headed into the boards. He had time to adjust, though, and raised his knees so that his skates took the impact. He was fine. Mr. Dillinger could always fix the lost edge on a pair of skates; he couldn't fix a broken ankle.

Nish held his temper. But the player who had hit him did not. He started yelling and cursing at the referee – until the ref raised his arm again and blew his whistle long and loud.

He was being thrown out of the game!

The Owls all gathered at the bench, watching the lunacy unfold. A single goal had been scored, and already one player was being thrown out. Travis looked over at the Cheetahs' bench. The coach – Butch Ruby – was scowling, but behind him a slightly hunched man in a Cheetahs team jacket seemed in an absolute rage. He was up on the bench and had a water bottle in his hand.

Cursing loudly, the sharp-faced man threw the water bottle over the boards so it landed on the ice and went spinning fast toward the referee. A linesman blocked it with his skate and scooped up the bottle.

The referee blew his whistle again – bench penalty to the Cheetahs!

"Just stay here," Muck told them in a quiet voice. "Stay here and keep quiet. No lipping, no faces, nothing. They've already lost this game, and they know it."

Muck was right. With the big forward out of the game, they had lost much of their toughness. And now that their manager had thrown the water bottle, the Owls were handed a power play that turned into a 2–0 lead when Dmitri slipped up the right wing on a perfect pass from Sam, deked once, and rifled a backhander high into the net. The water bottle flew off and into the corner. Travis giggled, watching it spin as if in answer to the one thrown by their coach.

The Owls never looked back. With Muck telling them to make passes, stay clear of checks, and be patient, the Owls were soon up 3–0 on a goal from the point by, of all people, Fahd, the puck bouncing off several sticks and pads and skate blades before it somehow found its way into the net.

To the Cheetahs' credit, Butch Ruby called a time out and instructed his players to play hockey for the rest of the match. They took the score to 3–2, but then the Owls went ahead 5–2 on a goal by Sarah on a gorgeous end-to-end rush, and one by big Andy Higgins on a booming slapper from the right circle.

The game ended 5–3. The Owls all lined up to shake hands. Some of the Cheetahs seemed reluctant to join in, even though both teams had been told that the end-of-game handshake was a tournament rule. Butch Ruby pushed two of the reluctant players toward the line, and very deliberately he walked up to Muck with his hand out. The two old junior players shook hands warmly, Butch slapping Muck on the back for his victory.

Travis couldn't help noticing that the Cheetahs' manager, the sharp-faced guy who'd angrily thrown the water bottle, was refusing to join the line, even though Mr. Dillinger was out in his sneakers and sliding along as he congratulated each player.

The man seemed furious. His face was a dark storm of twisting emotions – almost as if he wanted to go out and settle the game with his bare hands.

Travis shuddered. There was something horrible about the man's attitude. Muck would never have tolerated behavior like that, and Travis wondered why Butch Ruby did. From what he'd seen of Muck and Butch together, it was apparent that Muck liked the Kansas coach. Why, then, this awful little man in the Cheetahs jacket?

"We were lucky," Muck said in the dressing room as the Owls relaxed and took off their equipment. "If they hadn't acted stupid in that first shift, we would have had a 3–3 game that could have gone in either direction."

"They should be called the *Cheaters*," said Sam. "What a bunch of dirty players!"

"Not all," Muck said. "They showed they can play, too, after that opening foolishness. I wouldn't be surprised if we met them again before this is over."

Travis felt the same. He undressed slowly.

Nish was mumbling about heading out to a store to buy some "regulation" straws – *whatever that meant* – but Travis just wanted to be quiet and take in his surroundings.

Mr. Dillinger was already sharpening skates when Travis and Sarah decided to check out the arena facilities. They took in the indoor soccer pitch, the weight room, the restaurant, and the snack bar, and they were just about to head out to connect again with the rest of the team when it happened.

Slap! . . .

SLAP!

There are some sounds that are simply unmistakable. Thunder. A train rattling through a crossing. Tires losing traction in the snow. And skin slapping hard on skin.

Startled, Sarah and Travis stopped short. They were near a dressing-room door that was held open slightly by a wedge of hockey tape between door and frame – just enough for them to peek in.

The Cheetahs' manager was standing in front of a player. With his hunched stance, the man looked like a hawk staring down his prey.

The player had his helmet off, but both Travis and Sarah knew instantly who he was: the player who had been tossed out of the game for his nasty hit on Nish.

The anger Travis had seen earlier in the manager's eyes was being directed at the youngster. So intense and furious was the stare that it seemed entirely conceivable that the kid might burst into flames.

Instead, he just sat there, slumped in his chair.

It looked like the manager's hand had been branded on his cheek.

Travis looked at Sarah. The manager walked over, kicked the hockey tape out from the door frame, and slammed the door shut, though they were certain he hadn't noticed them.

They stood in the corridor, not knowing what to do.

"We'd better tell Muck," Sarah said.

"First chance we get," said Travis.

7

"What's he doing now?"

Travis didn't have to ask who "he" was. Who else could it be? Travis and Sarah, still shaken by what they'd witnessed – no, not actually *witnessed*, but what they *knew* had happened in that dressing room – had come out to the area in front of the rink where the players would be picked up by their various billets. Some of the Owls were already gone, but there was still a gang surrounding Nish: Fahd, Jeremy, Dmitri, Data,

Simon, Derek, Jesse, Lars, Sam, and a few others.

They couldn't quite see what Nish was up to, but they really didn't have to, as Data, the team's official statistician, was counting off numbers.

"Seventy-three.

"Seventy-four.

"Seventy-five.

"Seventy-six . . ."

Travis and Sarah edged in. Nish had several large packages of straws, the smaller ones from the grocery store rather than the large, thick ones you get when you buy a drink at a fast-food restaurant, and he was stuffing the straws into his mouth as fast as he could, some of them falling to the ground as he worked.

Data, ever the perfectionist, did a masterful job of subtracting the dropped ones even as he counted.

"Eighty-two.

"Eighty-one.

"Eighty-two.

"Eighty-three . . ."

Nish was making snorting noises through the straws. He sounded like the pigs Travis liked to watch at the Tamarack Fall Fair. Nish grunted and snorted and breathed so hard it seemed he might pass out from lack of oxygen, but he was not stopping.

"Give it up, Big Mouth," Sam called out. "You're going to need more than a hockey puck to stretch that ugly mug of yours – how about just putting your foot in it like you usually do?"

Even preoccupied, Nish glared at Sam, his eyes flashing with annoyance. Sam just laughed.

Finally, with one huge choke that sounded like a car backfiring, Nish spat the straws out, and they flew through the air like Pick-Up Sticks. He scrambled to retrieve them, Fahd and Dmitri helping him stuff the hundred or more straws back into the boxes they'd come in.

"You were fifty-seven short," Data announced with authority. "You had ninety-four in your mouth, by my count – the world record is 151."

"I'll do it!" Nish sputtered, the red draining from his face. "I can do it. I just need more practice."

"You need a psychiatrist," Sarah said matter-of-factly.

Nish blew a huge raspberry at her, spittle flying much like the straws had moments earlier.

"Very dignified," Sarah said, as she walked off. "Very classy, as usual."

Nish was furious, but he held his temper. He had his straws to collect.

Travis also had things to do. He caught up to Sarah, who had headed for a bench to sit on and wait for her ride.

She was clutching her arms around herself as if she were cold, but it was so hot in Texas that Mr. Dillinger had said he could have fried an egg on his bald spot.

"You okay?" Travis said.

Sarah seemed near tears. "Did you see his face?"

"Yeah. You could see exactly where the hand hit him."

Sarah shook her head. "I don't mean that. I mean, did you see how terrified he was?"

"I guess," Travis answered.

"It makes no sense," Sarah said. "The kid wasn't crying. He wasn't turning away. He just took it. Just sat there and took it. *Why?*"

"I don't know what you mean."

"What kind of hold can someone have over a kid that he could stand there and do something like that and the kid would be too scared to even move? There's something weird there, don't you think?"

Travis certainly did. Coaches and team managers didn't hit their players. There were laws against it. He'd heard of adults being kicked out of hockey for doing mean things to the kids they were in charge of. But he wasn't sure he knew what Sarah meant. She was talking almost as if the Cheetahs' manager had a spell over that big kid.

"When should we tell Muck?" Travis asked.

"We can't right now," Sarah said, waving to a car that was just pulling in. "My billet's here. Before tomorrow's game, though. Okay?"

"Okay."

8

The Owls were to meet at the rink at ten the following morning. Once again, Travis's billet, Mr. Finebester, was slow getting them there – he drove slower, Travis was convinced, than his grand-mother drove down the single-lane road to the cottage – so the rest of the team had already gathered by the time Mr. Finebester pulled up to the arena, though *crept up* might have been more accurate.

"What's going on?" asked Derek. He was squashed in the middle of the backseat.

Travis could see the Screech Owls all standing around Nish. Nish had his arms raised in the air like he had just won an Olympic gold medal. His mouth was bloated with straws.

As Travis and the others piled out of Mr. Finebester's car, Fahd shouted.

"He's got it! Nish has beaten the world record!"

"*The heck he has!*" shouted back Sam, who was standing to the side. "We should trade him to the Cheetahs – he's totally *cheating*!"

Nish was now strutting triumphantly around the drop-off area in front of the Northwoods ice rink. Fahd was taking photographs of the historic moment with his cell phone. Nish's mouth was stuffed, for sure – *packed*, would be more like it – but could Nish possibly have made up the shortfall that Data had calculated just the day before? Nish hadn't even been able to reach 100. Data had said he was still fifty-seven short, hadn't he?

Nish used both hands to grasp the straws like a megaphone. He carefully drew the stack out of his mouth and smacked his lips to wet them again. He seemed stunningly pleased with himself.

"152!" Nish announced as if he were calling a bingo game. "152 straws in one mouth, ladies and gentlemen. A new Guinness world record. And you all are my witnesses!"

"We'll have to sign a paper verifying it really happened," said Fahd.

"*I'm not signing nothing!*" shouted Sam. "*He cheated!*"

"Did not!" Nish sputtered.

"I counted," Fahd said in his best teacher's voice. "And it was 152. The *old* world record was 151."

"He *cheated*," insisted Sam.

"I don't know what to say," added Data. "Yes, there were 152 straws – but I don't know whether he followed regulations . . ."

"*Regulations?*" Nish roared, his face now an overripe tomato. "What regulations? The old world record holder – who can even remember his name now? – put 151 straws in his mouth. Wayne Nishikawa just put 152 straws in his mouth. We have photographic evidence" – he pointed at Fahd, who held up his cell phone as if that proved it – "and we have more than a dozen witnesses."

"Oh, come on, Nish," said Sam, shaking her red hair violently. "Get off the pot! You *cheated* and you know it."

"What's she mean?" Travis asked.

"Just check the straws," Sam said.

Travis thought she meant he should count them. But she meant something else. She went over and pulled the straws from Data's hands. She gripped them firmly and turned them over, shaking hard.

Straws spilled down by the dozen.

But how could they if Sam was holding the bundle tight?

"He put small straws inside the big ones," Sam explained. "And in some cases, smaller straws inside those. That's cheating, in my book!"

Data shook his head. "Probably in Guinness's book, too."

"Whaddya mean?" said Nish, livid now.

"You can't win on a technicality," Data explained. "It's obvious you have to pack the straws beside each other to win. You can't have little straws inside bigger ones. It's not right."

"It's cheating," Sam corrected.

"She's right," said Sarah, before Travis could agree. "I'm sure Guinness would insist the straws all be of one size and not inside each other. It only makes sense."

Nish could see he was losing the battle. He kicked the straws violently, sending them spinning along the walkway and over the curb.

He began to walk into the rink, but not before turning quickly to scream at Sam. "*You're such a total jerk, you know!*"

"Takes one to know one."

"You wait. I'll do it. I'll break that world record before we leave here."

Nish stormed toward the door and yanked it open, but he paused again to direct one more furious look at Sam.

"And," he added, "I'll be tournament MVP – guaranteed."

"I'll have a word with Butch."

Muck had calmed them down, as he always did. Sarah and Travis had gone to the coach before their second game and asked if they could speak privately to him. Muck nodded and, limping slightly on his bad leg, led them away from the dressing room toward the rink area, where he leaned back against the glass and waited.

"Well?" he said, after Travis and Sarah hesitated.

They told him. About the slap, about looking through the crack in the door, about the fury in the face of the Cheetahs' manager, and about the reaction of the player who had been booted out of the game.

"You *heard* a slap?" Muck said very slowly when they had finished. "You didn't *see* it?"

Both shook their heads. Muck squeezed his nose and looked up, thinking.

"What do you think it was all about?" he asked them.

Again they shook their heads. They didn't know. Travis took a guess: "He was upset because the kid got kicked out of the game?"

"Maybe," Muck said. "I saw him on the bench. He seemed far more upset at the officials than at the player. I'll talk to Butch about this."

Travis and Sarah smiled, grateful to be relieved of the burden of knowing this terrible thing, and glad that Muck – who would know exactly what to do – was taking over.

Muck patted them both gently on their backs and nudged them toward the dressing room.

"We have a game to play."

And what a game! The Owls' second opponents of the San Antonio Peewee Invitational were the Minnesota Moose. Mr. Dillinger gave one of his comical pregame pep talks, this one about how these kids had grown up just like the Screech Owls, except they had it harder: "In Minnesota, winters are so cold you have to breathe through your mouth 'cause your nostrils are locked tight.

"These are tough kids. They learned the game on frozen ponds using horse dung for pucks. They used old catalogs for shin pads, and some of them skated on hunting knives. I hear some of them walked five miles uphill to get to school and five miles uphill to get back –"

"That makes no sense," said Fahd, who never seemed to know when someone was being serious or not.

"Huh?" said Mr. Dillinger, looking surprised.

"How could they walk uphill both ways?"

"Fahd!" Sam giggled. "He's pulling our legs."

"What's dung?" Nish asked out of the blue.

"What?" said Mr. D, this time genuinely surprised.

"It's poop!" Lars said. "Even I know that. People used to use frozen horse poop for pucks – my dad says they even did that in Sweden."

"What a stink!" Nish offered, pinching his nose.

"Man, but you're an idiot!" Sam said. "Frozen stuff doesn't smell. You ever stick your head in your parents' freezer?"

"Probably several times a day!" said Dmitri. The whole team was now laughing at Nish.

"Sounds gross," Nish said, and went back to putting new tape on Ol' Betsy.

The Minnesota Moose were almost as good as Mr. D had advertised. They played like Canadians: fast, tough in the corners, determined, and quiet. No trash talk to fire up Nish. No dirty hooks or holding. Just hard hockey.

Travis didn't mind. He had skipped his first shot off the crossbar and was feeling like he was getting his legs. It wouldn't be long now before he wasn't even aware of skating.

Derek Dillinger put the Owls ahead late in the first period when he intercepted a Moose pass near center ice, split the backpedaling defense, and put in his own rebound after the Moose goalie made a fine diving save that put him down and out, unable to stop Derek's second shot.

The Moose tied it in the second when Fahd tried to hit Jesse with a long pass out from his own end and a tall Moose player gloved the puck down, passing quickly to a winger, who tipped the puck in behind Jenny, who had no chance.

Muck was changing lines fast to put the Owls' speed to good advantage. The Moose coach was trying to match lines, anxious to get his best skaters and checkers out against Sarah's line.

Nish was blocking shots wonderfully, using his big body and pads to act almost as a second goaltender for Jenny. He went down on a hard slapper from the point and took it right in the mask, but he still managed to cuff the puck with his glove over to Travis, who wheeled quickly and backhanded a pass off the boards that Sarah picked up just behind the Moose defense.

Sarah didn't even look. She knew exactly what Dmitri would be doing, blasting full out for the Moose blue line. She floated a pass perfectly and he caught it on the fly, just onside, and broke in alone for – no surprise – a forehand deke, fake shot, back to the backhand, and high into the net, the water bottle spinning off.

The referee's whistle was screaming. Travis turned and saw the ref signaling no goal. He turned hard and skated toward the referee, his hands held out helplessly.

"Wasn't offside!" Travis protested.

"Didn't call it offside," the referee said. "Player down."

Travis looked back. Mr. D was being helped by Fahd and Sam toward a downed player on the ice.

Travis could see the number: 44. It was Nish.

Mr. D had a towel and his first-aid kit. Sliding and lurching, he made it to Nish as quickly as possible with the support of the two Owls. Travis and his linemates skated back quickly.

There was blood on the ice. Nish's helmet was off, and Mr. D pressed the towel hard to Nish's mouth.

Nish wanted up. He struggled and got to one knee, Mr. D still holding the towel tight to his face. Nish pulled the towel away and began skating toward the bench.

All the players on the ice, and all the players sitting in the boxes, rapped their sticks on the ice in salute. The big defenseman who had taken the slapper that Nish had blocked skated over quickly and tapped Nish on the shin pads. The hockey apology. He hadn't meant to hurt him.

Travis liked what he was seeing. A tough team, but not a dirty one.

The game resumed after the arena attendants had scraped up as much of Nish's blood as they could.

The Moose had the puck deep in the Owls' end. Jenny made a blocker save and the puck bounced out to Dmitri. Travis didn't have to think. They had worked this play a hundred times in practice. Dmitri had it on his backhand and lifted the puck high over the heads of the Moose players, almost hitting the clock.

Everyone watched the puck sail. Everyone but Travis. He didn't need to see a thing to know where it would land. He heard a hard slap on the ice beside him as he crossed center: Dmitri's lob pass, perfectly delivered.

Travis kicked the puck up onto his stick and saw nothing but open ice, the Moose goalie coming out to challenge and then, as Travis crossed the blue line, wiggling hard back to keep his angle on Travis's shot. Travis raised his stick for the slapper and the goalie dropped into his butterfly, convinced he hadn't given Travis anything to shoot at.

He hadn't. But Travis had hoped for exactly this. He faked the shot, grabbed up the puck, and swept right around the now falling goalie to tuck the puck so sweetly into the back of the net it seemed he was nudging a rabbit into its cage.

The Owls had the lead, and they weren't going to give it up easily. The third period had barely begun when there was a great shuffle on the bench, everyone sliding down one, and Travis realized a big body had just come back on the far end, where the defense sat.

Nish was back.

Mr. Dillinger had fixed Nish's mask so it was back on the helmet, and Travis could see that Nish's badly swollen upper lip had a bandage on it.

Travis nodded to himself. There was Nish the total idiot, and there was Nish the total player. You never knew for sure which one you would get. But today it was obvious.

And they needed him. The Owls' one-goal lead held, but just barely, and only because of Nish's determination not to let any Moose players get a good shot away. The Moose came on hard in the third, pressing for the goal. They pulled their goalie late in the game, but it didn't work. Jesse Highboy, usually put on by Muck to do the checking, ended up with a goal when Jesse picked the pocket of the Moose's top player as he began what should have been the Moose's last rush.

The Owls had won 3–1 and were undefeated. The sparse crowd applauded, and the teams lined up to shake hands. No bad sports this time. The

Moose players were especially complimentary to Nish, who had his helmet off so everyone could have a good look at his stitched lip. Each Moose player gave his pads a special tap, and Nish was soaking up the attention.

"He's in his glory," Sarah said to Travis as they looked back.

"He deserves it," Travis said. "One of his best games ever."

"Agreed."

Nish was last into the dressing room. He came in as if he half-expected the Owls to have planned a surprise party for him, complete with cake, a speech by the mayor, and a special medal for bravery.

Mr. D was quick to puncture his balloon. "Great game, Nishikawa," he said. "Just be thankful those kids no longer play with frozen horse dung!"

"Why not go for *that* world record, Nish," Sam shouted out. "Most horse poop in a human mouth!"

Nish was now a furious shade of red. He tossed his helmet into his locker.

"*I'm going to hurl!*" he said.

At least that's what Travis thought his friend had said.

It actually sounded like "*Mmmm gna herr!*"

There were some advantages to having Nish's mouth stitched shut.

10

Muck wanted to see Travis and Sarah. He asked the two Owls to step aside for a few minutes while the other players were being collected by their various billets.

Muck seemed troubled. He limped down to where the Zamboni chute exited outside and the two players followed him. He rubbed his hands together as if warming them. A strange thing to do in weather that was nearing 100 degrees Fahrenheit.

"I spoke with Butch," Muck told them. He seemed to be searching for words.

"Butch says the manager is new to the team. His name is Jimmy Vim, and he apparently is very rich. He's the one who put up the money for their bus. He sponsors the team and pays for everything. I'm not so sure Butch is comfortable with the arrangement, but the parents voted for it, so Butch feels helpless."

"What about the kid?" Sarah asked. "The kid he slapped?"

Muck pulled on his nose. "He's called Tanner Brady. Butch says he's new to the team, transferred over from a nearby town where he was a superstar. Apparently Jimmy Vim is acting as the kid's guardian. He has the parents' blessing, Butch says. Sort of hard on the kid, but Butch says he's actually a good lad – and a great player, so long as he holds his temper in."

"Is that how you check a kid's temper?" Sarah said. "By slapping his face?"

"Butch says he talked to the manager, and the guy says he slapped his hands together hard to emphasize a point he was making, that's all."

"We *saw* his face!" Sarah protested. "It was bright red!"

"But you told me you didn't actually *see* the slap."

"We didn't," Travis admitted. "But it was obvious what the guy had done."

"It's your word against his," Muck said. "And the kid isn't saying anything."

"He's too scared," said Sarah.

"Butch says he'll watch them closely. I don't think he's a great fan of this arrangement."

Sarah wasn't finished. She wanted to talk more about it, but the sound of a car honking caught their attention. It was Sarah's billet, waving for her.

"Better get going," Muck said. "We'll keep an eye on things, too."

The Owls had never had such a great evening. They dined along the River Walk at Casa Rio, a restaurant right on the water's edge at Commerce

Street, not far from the Alamo. It was a spectacular setting: palm trees, multicolored umbrellas, patio tables, and even tiny lizards darting about the tree trunks and songbirds in the branches.

"Amazing!" said Sam. "I'm never going home."

The Owls were given tables by the water so they could see the covered gondolas coming and going. There were even boats sailing by with full dinners being served on board as they made their way around the canals.

Before the Owls ordered their meals, they were given a welcome by the restaurant manager, a large man with a big mustache and a Mexican accent.

"Welcome to Casa Rio," he told them. "*Casa Rio* means 'River House' in Spanish. This is the oldest establishment on River Walk, but long, long before this restaurant, there was a bridge here, the main bridge over the San Antonio River. This was where the Mexican soldiers gathered on the morning of March 6, 1836. It was right about where you are sitting, young man" – he nodded toward Fahd, who pointed at himself with his eyebrows turning into question marks – "that the bugle call of El

Deguello was sounded. Anybody care to guess what that means, *El Deguello*?"

"Let's eat?" Nish offered.

The manager looked at Nish with pity. He was not amused. "No. It means 'Charge – with no quarter given.' No mercy. Total destruction. It meant they were attacking the Alamo, and there would be no prisoners taken. It is the cruelest bugle call of war."

The manager waited awhile for the reality of that to sink in. The Owls had seen where Davy Crockett and Jim Bowie and William Travis had fallen at the Alamo, but now they were seeing it from the other side, the Mexican army's side. Young soldiers would have been standing here – some almost as young as the Owls themselves – and they must have been terrified at the thought of having to attack until every single man defending the Alamo was dead. If they were to take no prisoners, they couldn't expect the men at the Alamo to show any mercy, either.

The manager smiled widely, his mustache bouncing, and changed the subject. "The chubby young man here," he said, pointing out the beet-faced Nish, "wants to eat. And we want to feed you. But first let me explain our menu . . ."

The Owls were familiar with some of the food. You could get nachos and fajitas and burritos in Tamarack out at the Taco Bell on the highway. And all of them had eaten chili. But this was so much more complicated, all this talk about refried beans and guacamole and tortillas. Travis was losing track of all the Mexican foods they could try.

"Let me tell you about our specialty," the manager said. "Stuffed jalapeños. Anyone here know what a jalapeño is?"

"A pepper," Data said.

"A hot pepper," the manager responded. "Hot, hot, hot. *Caliente*. Let me hear you say it in Spanish – *caliente*."

"*Caliente!*" the Owls shouted.

"Do not forget that word," he warned them. "Jalapeños aren't for everyone. These are sometimes so hot they can burn your skin just by touching them. You will feel your lips and tongue go numb. But if you only eat a little of them, and they are stuffed properly, they are the most delicious food in the world. Just make sure you have a tall glass of water beside you and, above all, if you touch one of the peppers, make sure you wash your hands quickly with soap and water. You got that? *Caliente.*"

The Owls loudly repeated the word: "*Caliente!*"

"Hot!" the manager said as a final warning.

The food was delicious. Travis sat at a table with Sarah, Sam, Dmitri, and Nish, and they ate everything the waiters brought. They even tried the stuffed jalapeños, but Sam spat hers out and downed half a glass of water, and Nish just left his sitting on his plate. Travis and Sarah and Dmitri ate theirs slowly and, so long as they washed each bite down with water, they tasted wonderful, and were even fun to eat.

"He's right," Sarah giggled. "I can't feel my lips."

"Just be careful," Travis warned.

"Well, look at that," a voice said from the next table. It was Lars. Everyone looked up to see a large boat come into view, the kind that served as a floating restaurant. It moved gracefully through the water and had a large canopy over it. There was a mariachi band on deck playing music, and as the large boat made its turn, the Owls were able to see who was on board.

It was the Cheetahs hockey team from Kansas City. Travis instantly recognized Butch Ruby, the coach, sitting off to the side enjoying the Mexican band. On the near side, sitting at a table together, were Tanner Brady – the big kid who had slammed into Travis and been kicked out of the game – and the Cheetahs' manager. What was his name again? Oh yeah, Jimmy Vim. Strange name.

"Watch this," Nish hissed.

He had taken the stuffed jalapeño and was packing it like a snowball.

Before Travis could say anything, Nish launched the stuffed pepper over the railing, and it splattered against an empty chair and rolled under the table where Jimmy Vim and Tanner Brady were sitting. Jimmy Vim heard the impact, spun around, and stared hard at the restaurant patio, where Nish's face was giving him away. Jimmy Vim pointed and yelled something, but the Owls couldn't make it out, and in an instant, the big boat was around the corner and slipping out of sight. Jimmy Vim stood at the back of the boat, shaking a fist at the kids sitting in the Casa Rio.

Nish was laughing so hard, Travis thought he'd explode.

"I'm gonna pee my pants," Nish announced.

"Good grief," Sam said. "You're disgusting."

"*I gotta run,*" Nish said, jumping up and scrambling toward the washrooms at the back of the restaurant.

Travis looked around. Muck and Mr. Dillinger were deep in conversation. They hadn't noticed anything.

"He's insane," Sam said.

"We know," Sarah said. "We've known since kindergarten."

Suddenly, the Owls' special meal was interrupted by a scream.

Mr. Dillinger and Muck stood up fast, almost knocking their table over.

Travis turned just in time to see Nish, his fly

wide open, come screaming from the washrooms, push past a waiter, race past Travis's table, and plunge over the restaurant railing. Headfirst into the San Antonio River.

When he surfaced, he was still screaming.

"What the heck's going on?" Mr. Dillinger shouted.

Sarah was laughing.

"What's so funny?" Travis asked her.

"Guess who forgot to wash his hands *before* he went to the bathroom?"

Instantly, Travis knew. Right before Nish raced off to the bathroom, he had been packing that jalapeño pepper like a snowball.

He would have had it all over his hands.

Caliente!

11

Nish walked gingerly from the parking area to the arena doors as if he were riding a horse. His beet-red face was already dripping with sweat – and he hadn't even put his equipment on yet.

"You gonna be okay to play?" Travis asked as Nish came in through the doors.

"Mr. D gave me some cream."

Nish looked a mess: lip still swollen from the stitches, face beaded with sweat, legs held wide enough apart for a kid on a tricycle to pass through.

But he was going to play.

Travis's awkward moment was saved by Sarah and Sam coming fast along the corridor. Sarah seemed baffled; Sam looked angry.

"What's up?" Travis called to them.

"You're not going to believe this," Sam said, shaking her head.

"Come with us," Sarah instructed.

Travis turned to Nish, who seemed not the slightest bit interested in what the girls had found out. "You go ahead," Nish told Travis. "I'm going to get dressed early."

Travis moved along with the girls, puzzled by their air of mystery.

They passed the Owls' dressing room and stopped at a little side room where Mr. D had set up his portable skate sharpener. As always, the Owls' manager had laid everything out perfectly, tools all squared up, sharpener ready to go, skates lined up in order for sharpening.

"Sure seems to be a lot of skates," Travis said, as he glanced around.

"They're the Cheetahs' skates," Sam said.

"What're they doing here? This is Mr. D's room."

Just then, Mr. Dillinger himself backed through the swinging door to the room, carrying an armful of skates – *more* skates.

"What's going on?" Sarah demanded.

Mr. D, always in a good humor, just chuckled. "I guess I'm now the equipment manager for the Cheetahs, too."

"Why are you doing their skates?" said Travis.

"Because they asked me to," Mr. D shrugged, setting down the skates and lining each pair up in his usual orderly fashion. He stopped and scratched his bald spot.

"Their manager says their machine isn't working right. But I don't think he knows how to sharpen skates, actually. When I let him bring the first pile of skates in, I started lining them up in pairs and told him to go ahead with the first batch – but it was pretty clear he hadn't a clue."

"Some manager!" Sam said with disgust.

"Ah, not everyone can sharpen," Mr. D said. "It's an art – and I'm the best there is, don't you know."

He laughed harder at his own little joke than the kids did, then happily went about sharpening the rest of the Cheetahs' skates. He carefully set the first skate up, ran the blade across the grinder – sparks flying – and then stopped.

"He is a strange one, Jimmy Vim, I have to admit. But if you can't help out another hockey team, what good are you?"

"I'd grind their blades down to nothing," growled Sam.

"Oh, now, now, now," chided Mr. D, returning to his task.

The kids headed back to the dressing room together. To get there, they had to pass the dressing room where the Kansas City team would be getting ready for their next game later in the day.

"Let's see if they even have a sharpener," Sam said, pushing open the door.

"We'll get caught!" Sarah said.

"Nah – c'mon," Sam said, stepping in. The others followed, Travis's heart pounding so loud he thought the girls would hear it.

The Cheetahs' bags were piled in a heap in the center of the room. Mr. D would have already set out the bags in front of each player's stall, their names thumbtacked to the top so there could be no doubt where each team member sat and where each of the numbered equipment bags should go.

"This guy's a team manager?" Sam asked in despair.

"Over there," Travis pointed. "I bet that's their sharpener."

But it was impossible to say. Mr. D's portable sharpener folded up to pack neatly into a small bag. And it was carefully labeled "Sharpener – Property of the Screech Owls" so there could be no mistake.

This was a padlocked metal box, and heavy – Travis had trouble budging it – with no label on it whatsoever.

"I bet they don't even have a sharpener," Sam said. "I bet he lied to Mr. D so he'd do his work for him."

"Why would anyone want to be the manager

of a hockey team if he didn't know what he was doing?" Sarah asked.

"Who knows?" said Travis. "Look at the way he treats that kid – and apparently it's not even his son."

"He's only manager because he pays for everything – like that fancy bus," added Sam. "I hate this team."

Travis giggled. "You can't hate them – you don't even know them."

"I hate them. I hate their manager. I hate the kid."

"Well, get used to them," Travis warned. "Muck is convinced we're going to meet them again if we make the final."

The Owls were about to leave when they noticed a poster taped to the far wall. It was slightly battered and torn, as if it had been repeatedly taped up then taken down in whatever dressing room the Cheetahs happened to be in.

Sam read it aloud:

I am the master of my fate;
I am the captain of my soul.

"What's that supposed to mean?" Travis asked.

"No idea," said Sam. "No idea at all."

The Screech Owls played the Oklahoma City Ice Breakers later in the morning. Nish played, but not well. Travis could only shake his head and wonder how he could even play at all. He seemed slow and tender, and didn't go down to block any shots. Fortunately, Dmitri was having a terrific game, twice roofing backhands as he came down on his off wing and cut across to draw the Ice Breakers' goalie out.

Travis had a fine game himself, once scoring on a breakaway after Sarah sent him a long pass straight up over center ice, and later making a nifty back pass to Lars at the point, who shot a bullet that clipped in under the crossbar.

The game finished with the Owls up 5–1. The victory put them into the next round, giving them only two hours' break before a big match against the Dallas Shooting Stars. The winner would advance to the championship game.

"Let's get some lunch," Travis said to Nish as they dropped off their sticks and headed for their stalls to undress.

"Bring me a milkshake, will you?" Nish said. "I'm just going to wait here until the game."

Travis was about to argue but then thought better of it. "Okay," he said. "But take your jersey off and let it dry. You don't want to catch a cold."

Nish set about taking off his jersey and shoulder and elbow pads while Travis and the rest of the Owls slipped out of their gear and into their tracksuits. Travis set off to the tuckshop, where he picked up an egg salad sandwich, an orange drink, and, after he had finished, a chocolate milkshake for Nish.

"Where are your straws?" Travis asked looking around as he was handed the shake.

"Oh, sorry," said the woman running the cash. "We've had to keep them back here." She reached behind the register to get a straw for Travis. "Some stupid kid was helping himself to them to the point where we ran completely out."

The two hours passed quickly. Nish was first dressed, slipping his shoulder and elbow pads, then jersey, back on before anyone else could even get out of their tracksuits. Mr. Dillinger quietly closed the door, the signal that Muck was about to give one of his rare talks to the team.

"The Cheetahs won their game 8–1," Muck began. "Seems the kids never had such good skate sharpening before." Muck turned and looked hard at Mr. D, whose eyebrows and mustache seemed to leap together in mock surprise.

"They get a bye into the championship, meaning the winner of this game will meet them tomorrow. We beat them once; I think we can take them again, but first we have to get past this Dallas team, and I want your full concentration on the task at hand – you got that, Nishikawa?"

Nish sat with his head nearly on his knees. He nodded, never looking up.

"This team is strong and quick," Muck

continued. "They have one kid with a cannon from the point, so if you're going to block shots, make sure you go down right and position yourself properly. If you can't block it, get the heck out of the way so the goalie can see the shot. Understand, Nishikawa?"

Nish nodded again. He knew how poorly he had played against Oklahoma City. He hadn't blocked a single shot. And they had scored off a shot that ticked in off Nish's stick as he stood in front of Jenny, seeming unsure what to do.

"Let's go, then," Muck said quietly.

"LET'S GO OWLS!" Mr. D shouted, opening the door.

"GO OWLS!" the players shouted as they rose and hurried to the door, grabbing their sticks from the rack as they passed.

Travis felt good. The ice had just been flooded, so it glistened like polish. There was still enough water that he could hear his skates sizzle on the first corner. He hit the crossbar on his very first try.

There was something different this time about Nish. Right from the opening face-off, he was a new player. More accurately, he was the *old* Nish: charging up the ice, rubbing Dallas forwards out along the boards if they tried to beat him to the outside, dropping in front of pucks.

Travis had to admire Muck's coaching strategies. Muck sometimes seemed to control Nish as if Nish came with switches and buttons and Muck knew exactly which one to push or flick on or off. Two little jabs in the dressing room and Nish was transformed.

But Travis knew how hard this was for Nish. He had seen the pain that Nish was in when he arrived at the rink.

With the score tied 1–1 in the second period, Nish gathered the puck back of his own net. He stood there, swaying side to side as he tried to sucker the Dallas forechecker into chasing him so that he could use the net by slipping out the other side, away and free.

The checker fell for it, darting hard behind the net. Nish calmly tapped the puck forward off the back bar of the goal, the checker passing by so fast he had no time to react.

Nish gathered up the puck as it bounced back to him and took off on the free side. He was skating hard, head up, hands soft, and puck silently moving on the blade of his stick – the sure sign of a player with good hands.

He slipped the puck right between the skates of the first Dallas player up to try and check him.

Sarah slammed her stick hard on the ice. Nish heard and slipped a perfect pass to her as she broke over center.

Sarah's intention was to split the defense. She picked up more speed and tried to jump through as the two Dallas defenders closed the gap. Sarah spun off one player and into the other, all three falling down.

Nish was in quick to grab the puck. In desperation, one of the Dallas defenders swung his stick from the ice, catching Nish just above the ankles.

Nish was airborne. But somehow he still had the puck on his stick and miraculously got away a shot even as he was flying hard into the corner boards. The goaltender trapped the puck between his glove arm and his side, but it seemed to scurry through like a frightened mouse, plopping just over the line for a goal.

Travis raced to Nish, lying crumpled on the ice. He was obviously in pain. Travis leaned over to help his friend up.

Nish had given the Owls a lead they never lost. With the big defenseman playing his heart out, the Dallas Shooting Stars shot blanks. They couldn't get by Nish, who fell in front of any shot they attempted. If a player went into a corner with Nish, it was Nish who always came out of the corner with the puck.

The Owls won 7–1, with Nish once again chosen Player of the Game. He had been the star in two of the three games the Owls had played.

Nish just might, Travis thought, end up as he had predicted: MVP of the tournament.

12

"You know what you have to do."

Travis shot a glance at Sarah. She was bending over, pretending to retie her skate laces, having great difficulty holding in a laugh. He knew why. Muck's big speech before the championship game in the San Antonio Peewee Invitational had amounted to *seven* words.

"You know what you have to do," Muck repeated, standing in the center of the dressing room. As he spoke he then turned slowly in a full circle, staring into the eyes of every single one of the Screech Owls.

Travis could have sworn Muck lingered a moment when he got to Nish, but if he did pause, it was just for a second. Perhaps Muck was trying to figure out why his star defenseman insisted on wearing that stupid Davy Crockett cap. Perhaps he just wanted to stare long enough to send his big red-faced defenseman a telepathic message: "*You hear me, Nishikawa? You know what you have to do. That means no goofing around, no all-star plays, no sulking, no stupid penalties, no hotdogging, no lipping off at the refs, no chirping at the other team's bench . . .*"

There would be no need for words, though. Travis knew his friend too well. This was the championship game. The Screech Owls were up against the Kansas City Cheetahs, just as Muck had predicted would happen. The two best teams in the tournament were meeting for the second time, winner take all. The United States against Canada – just like in the Olympics.

Travis pulled on his jersey, kissing it just as the *C* slipped past his mouth on the way to its position over his heart. He was ready to go.

Only a few times in his life had Travis felt such intensity on the ice. The rink was packed, as most of the teams that were out of the tournament had arranged to stay for the whole championship in case they happened to reach the final. The stands were filled with peewee hockey players, their parents, their billets, and a huge number of supporters that had driven down from Kansas City. There were even cheerleaders wearing the Cheetahs' colors and men waving huge flags with the Cheetahs' logo on them. The Owls had never felt so alone in all their hockey lives.

But as Muck often said, hockey games weren't won in the stands. Travis remembered the coach's big pregame speech; he knew what he had to do. He would get into his own zone, and it would be as if a cone of silence had come over him, the blur and sounds of the rink unable to penetrate and distract him. His concentration would be solely on the ice, in the play. At times like this, he liked to think of himself as hockey equipment, not human.

Nish was clearly in his zone. It was as if he didn't even see Travis when Travis skated by and whacked his shin pads just before the opening face-off. Same for Sarah. She was inside herself, breathing deep as she stood with her stick across her knees, waiting for the referee to come to the face-off circle with the puck. Dmitri, on the far wing, was set perfectly. Travis often thought that if a scientist and an architect were to design the perfect hockey player, it would be Dmitri. He never looked anything but perfectly set, almost as if he'd been born with skates on his feet and a stick in his hands.

"*I owe you one,*" the winger opposite Travis growled.

Travis didn't acknowledge his presence. He knew who it was: Tanner Brady. He felt the discreet little slash over his stick delivered by the winger as they approached the face-off. He ignored him completely. There would be plenty of time in the game to get to know Tanner Brady.

The fans were screaming for the Cheetahs.

Travis blocked it out. He looked quickly at the Cheetahs' bench. The coach, Butch Ruby, was standing behind the players, hands stuffed into his jacket pockets. The manager, Jimmy Vim, was standing *on* the bench, arms folded, challenging.

It struck Travis as odd. He had never seen a team manager stand on a bench before. He couldn't imagine Mr. D ever acting like that. What was with this guy?

"*Gonna crush you!*" the voice opposite growled as Travis's stick was lightly slashed again.

Travis said nothing in return. He would let his play answer for him.

The puck dropped, and Sarah plucked it out of the air just before it hit the circle. She swept it back to Fahd, who moved it cross-ice to Nish. Travis cut for the center, rapping his stick once on the ice to let Nish know he was clear. Nish hit him perfectly with a tape-to-tape pass, and Travis backhanded a shot hard off the center-ice boards.

It was a play they had talked about trying earlier in the day if they got a chance. Travis would drive across center, and Sarah and Dmitri would race for the opposition blue line. Travis would then use the boards to get the puck past any checkers and have it ricochet into the opposition end just ahead of a charging Dmitri.

Dmitri read the play exactly and picked up Travis's banked pass as he hit the right circle. He then curled sharp and fed it to Sarah, coming in hard down the slot.

Sarah faked a shot by dipping her shoulder, and the Cheetahs' goaltender went for it. He fell to his knees, butterfly position, and readied to block or catch the shot – but the shot never came. Sarah paused on her snap shot and instead picked up the puck again and deftly swept around the goalie and tucked it into the open side of the net.

Screech Owls 1, Cheetahs 0 – first shot of the game, first minute of the game.

Travis had half-expected to be hammered into the boards once he got the puck to Dmitri, but there was no check or slash. He turned and saw Tanner Brady heading back to try and help his defense out – as he should have been doing. He got there just a moment too late.

Travis's line went off, and Derek Dillinger's line came out. The Cheetahs also switched lines, and while Travis was catching his breath, he saw Jimmy Vim cuff the back of Tanner Brady's helmet and shove him hard. Butch Ruby, the coach, saw it and said nothing, though Travis thought he could see disgust on Butch's face. It was hard to say. Perhaps Butch was disgusted at the way the Cheetahs' top line had let the Owls score so early and easily.

The Cheetahs tied the score later in the opening period when Tanner Brady picked up a loose puck in the neutral zone, came over the blue line on Fahd's side, and blasted a slap shot right between Fahd's legs. The quick, screened shot fooled Jeremy, who was looking for the pass, and it went in under his blocker on the short side.

Nice play, Travis thought. The kid can play, when he's not out there gooning it up.

Heading into the third period, it was 3–3, Jesse Highboy having tipped a blast, delivered by Nish from the point, in behind the Cheetahs' goaltender – and Nish himself having scored when he joined the rush, picked up a drop pass left for him by Derek, danced around the defenseman, and then tossed a backhand high into the net, Dmitri style, as he fell and crashed into the boards.

Travis wasn't sure Nish needed to crash into the boards after scoring, but he knew his friend well enough to know that Nish might have felt a little dramatic effect wouldn't hurt. Travis turned to see what Sarah thought, and she rolled her eyes in answer.

The second and third Kansas City goals came from great individual plays by the big winger, Tanner Brady. He was a force on the ice, for sure. In the second goal, he carried the puck end to end and lofted a perfect saucer pass over Sam's stick to give his center an easy one-timer that beat Jeremy. For the third goal, which tied the game, he picked Fahd's pocket by lifting the Screech Owl's stick just as Fahd was about to pass up to Travis, then turned with the puck and fired a hard shot at Jeremy, which Jeremy brilliantly blocked by throwing his body across the net. The rebound came straight back to the shooter, and with Jeremy out of position, Tanner had an empty cage to toss the puck into.

They flooded between the second and third periods – just like in the NHL. Travis came back out early to the bench, just in time to catch Jimmy Vim tearing a strip off Tanner Brady, who so far had been the hero of the game for the Cheetahs.

The Cheetahs' manager was screaming at his star player and holding him by the scruff of his neck so he was face-to-shield with him. Travis, wearing his own helmet, could only pick up a few of the shouted words: "*. . . win this period or else . . . screw this up and the deal's off, understand? . . . take that big defenseman out if you get a chance, you hear?*"

Jimmy Vim shut up when the rest of the Cheetahs came out with their coach. Travis was certain this time that he saw a look in Butch Ruby's eyes that said he didn't approve of his manager's behavior. But why didn't he do something?

The third period started off fast – the ice slick, the two teams tied and knowing the championship would soon be settled. Travis's line started again and had a good shift, though no scoring chances.

Nish was playing as only Nish could under such circumstances. He was all over the ice, blocking shots, breaking up rushes, leading rushes, and even though he was quick to join the rush when the Owls had the puck and were attacking, he was even quicker to get back if the puck was turned over and the Cheetahs attacked.

Travis noticed blood oozing from Nish's stitched lip. He must have taken a stick in the mouth. But he'd said nothing. There'd been no dramatics. On another day, he might have fallen to the ice and flailed around like he'd just been struck by lightning in the hopes of drawing a penalty. Not this time. This time, Nish was all business.

The other impressive player was Tanner Brady. He, too, seemed all over the ice. He played hard but not dirty. He looked exhausted, his jersey soaked from sweat, but he never quit.

Something had to give. The Owls struck first when Nish blocked a shot, quickly got to his feet, and fired the puck up to a breaking Dmitri, who flew down the ice and cut across the net, spinning completely around in a move that dazzled the poor Cheetahs' goaltender. Skating backwards, without even looking, Dmitri fired a backhander straight up into the roof of the net, sending the goalie's water bottle flying.

But the Cheetahs came right back, Tanner Brady carrying the puck up ice, evading a check from Jesse, and coming in hard on Sam, the last defense back. He looked like he was going to shoot, but instead lifted his stick, letting the sliding puck pass perfectly between the blades of Sam's skates. He slipped past her, gobbled up the puck again, and beat Jeremy high to the blocker side.

With seconds left in regular time, Travis had a glorious opportunity when Nish flicked a high pass toward the clock, and Travis – knowing the play so well now – raced ahead blind, knowing the puck would catch up to him. He had a clear breakaway from just outside the blue line, but he could not beat the Cheetahs' goaltender, who did the splits and just caught Travis's flick shot with the tip of his right pad.

When five minutes of overtime settled nothing, the organizers announced that the championship would be decided in a shootout.

"*Yes!*" Dmitri shouted on the bench.

"*Love it!*" cheered Sarah.

So did Travis. This was just like the NHL, just like the pros. He hoped Muck chose him as one of the three shooters. Then he hoped Muck wouldn't choose him. Then he hoped he would. He felt his heart jump with excitement and fear at the same time.

The coaches named their players. "Nishikawa," Muck told the referee. "Cuthbertson. Yakushev."

Travis's heart sank, and simultaneously he felt relief. The pressure was off. But he wanted so badly to be chosen, didn't he?

He felt Muck's big hand on his shoulder. The coach leaned over and spoke very quietly. "If it goes to extra shooters," Muck said. "I want you for it."

Good old Muck. Always saying the right thing. Always making sure players felt good about themselves.

Travis looked over at the Cheetahs' bench. The manager, Jimmy Vim, seemed to have a vise-grip hold on Tanner Brady's neck. It appeared to Travis as if he was squeezing hard and Tanner Brady was flinching but afraid to cry out. Jimmy Vim barked something into the player's ear.

Butch Ruby was listing his players to the official. Obviously Tanner Brady would be one of them.

The Cheetahs, as the designated "home" team, were given the choice of when to shoot. Butch Ruby chose first. He knew if they could score on the first chance, it might unnerve the Owls.

The first Cheetahs shooter tried to deke Jeremy but failed. Jeremy stayed with the puck and blocked any possible opening.

Nish shot first for the Owls. He came up ice as if he were out for a Sunday stroll with his grandmother, not a care in the world. He looked like he didn't realize he was in the spotlight, or that he even had the puck.

But suddenly, quick as a cat's paw, Nish's stick blade flicked the puck up high under the crossbar. The Cheetahs' goaltender hadn't even had time to move.

The Owls bench roared its approval, everyone leaning over to pound the boards with their sticks. Nish came back, red-faced and grinning, and knocked gloves down the entire line as he planted exaggerated kisses on Ol' Betsy, his faithful stick.

The Cheetahs' second shooter came in and whiffed on his shot, but as fate would have it, the puck kept sliding toward the net. Jeremy, convinced the shot had been going high, sprang up while the puck stayed low, and it just slipped in over the line.

Bad luck for the Screech Owls. The shootout was tied at one goal apiece.

Sarah shot next and tried to go five-hole, but the Cheetahs' goaltender was down in a perfect butterfly and his stick covered the small space between his pads.

The Cheetahs' third shooter was Tanner Brady. Travis saw the manager, Jimmy Vim, lean over and say something directly into his ear. He wished he knew what was being said. How strange, he thought, to see the team manager calling the shots while the coach stood to the side, watching suspiciously.

Tanner Brady picked up the puck at center ice and came in fast, stopping suddenly so hard in front of Jeremy that ice chips flew straight up and into the goalie's face. Jeremy, temporarily blinded, shook his head violently in an effort to throw off the snow – just as Tanner Brady curled a shot around his far side and into the net.

"*No fair!*" shouted Sam from the bench.

"*That's cheating!*" shouted Fahd.

Muck instantly put his hand on Fahd's shoulder to quiet him. Muck called over the referee, and they huddled for a few moments before the official backed off and Muck, looking none too pleased, nodded. The referee signaled "good goal" and pointed to center ice for the final shooter.

"He can't do that, can he?" Sam called over to Muck. Others were also calling out.

Muck shrugged. "So long as the puck continues to move forward and there's no body contact, I guess everything's fair." He seemed angry, but Travis knew his coach well enough to know Muck would keep it to himself.

Dmitri *had* to score for the shootout to continue – and if it continued, Travis knew he would be the next Owls shooter. He hoped so much that Dmitri would score, but also hoped – in a way that made no sense – that it wouldn't all come down to him.

Dmitri came in fast, stickhandling smoothly. He used his familiar deke – familiar to the Owls, not to the Cheetahs' goaltender – and the goalie fell for it, opening up the side.

Dmitri calmly moved to his backhand and lifted the puck high and hard, the Owls all watching, expecting the water bottle to go flying.

Only it didn't. The puck caught the crossbar and pinged loudly clear of the net.

The arena exploded. The Cheetahs' bench exploded. They had won the championship. And Tanner Brady was the hero.

Travis's heart sank.

There would be no night in the Alamo now.

13

As the two teams lined up for the medal presentations and the national anthem of the winning side, Travis's eyes were stinging. He stood proudly while "The Star-Spangled Banner" was played and the many Cheetahs fans in the stands loudly sang along. He liked the song fine – he actually knew the words better than the words of his own anthem – but he burned with a desire to hear "O Canada" and to be wearing a gold medal around his neck.

After the anthem, the organizer of the tournament took a microphone and moved to center ice.

He first announced the tournament all-star teams, as selected by the coaches of all the teams involved in the San Antonio Peewee Invitational.

Nish and Sarah both made first team, Sarah at center and Nish on defense. No surprise there. No surprise, either, that Tanner Brady was named the all-star winger.

The shock to Travis came when his teammates started pounding their sticks on the ice and someone cuffed his butt with a stick when they named the second team. He hadn't even heard his own name over the loudspeaker.

"Way to go, Trav!" Sarah shouted over the cheers.

"Awesome!" shouted Fahd.

How could that have happened? Travis wondered. He felt he hadn't played well enough to deserve such an honor. He had a few points – four goals and four assists – but he'd been more valuable defensively than offensively. He'd checked well and worked hard. Muck always said hard work would be rewarded, and he guessed this was proof

Muck was right. Coaches noticed such things, and coaches had selected the team.

"And now, ladies and gentlemen," said the tournament organizer, "we come to the tournament's Most Valuable Player, as selected by the media covering this magnificent event."

Travis stifled a giggle. "Media" meant one local neighborhood newspaper, but it sounded good. He'd seen the reporter around, a young woman who also had to take photographs for the paper. But she'd been at all the games, so why not ask her to choose?

"For the first time in the history of the San Antonio Peewee Invitational hockey tournament," the man announced, "we have a *tie* for MVP honors!" He paused while that sank in.

A tie for MVP? Travis had never heard of such a thing.

"Would Tanner Brady of the Kansas City Cheetahs please step forward?" the man announced, the loudspeaker squealing with feedback. "And, from the Tamarack Screech Owls . . . Wayne . . . Nish-Nisha-Nishi-caw-waw!"

Both teams erupted in cheers and stick-banging, and the fans in the stands applauded loudly as Tanner Brady and Nish – beet red from the announcer's hatcheting of his name – dropped their sticks and gloves and helmets and skated over to take their MVP trophies.

"*Go, Nish!*" Sam shouted.

"*NISH! NISH! NISH!*" the Owls chanted as one.

Nish skated to center ice, stopped on the face-off dot, and bowed to each side of the rink. Tanner Brady skated back to his team with his trophy, and for once he was given a hug by Jimmy Vim – but not before the Cheetahs' manager had thrown a scowl in Nish's direction.

The Owls were undressing when Muck came in. He congratulated them on a fine tournament and a great effort.

"I'm no fan of the shootout," he told them. "They might as well have the kids stand at center ice and play that paper-and-stone game."

Sam corrected him: "Rock-paper-scissors."

"Whatever," Muck continued. "Or flip a coin.

If you're playing a game that involves one *team* trying to score on another, you play till one team scores a proper goal – then you have your champion. But I don't make up the rules. Far as I'm concerned, if they could have two MVPs, they could have two champions."

Muck always said the right thing. How grateful Travis was to be playing for him and Mr. D, not Butch Ruby and that nutcase Jimmy Vim. Well, Butch might not be so bad, but Jimmy Vim struck Travis as a total sicko.

There was a knock at the door and Muck opened it. It was one of the organizers.

"Great game, kids," he said as he came through. "We've got some extra spaces tonight at the Alamo, if our tournament MVP here" – and with this he looked at a red-faced Nish – "and your two other all-stars would care to take them. It's a chance of a lifetime, kids – whaddya say?"

They were dumbstruck. Travis didn't like the idea of leaving the team – he was captain, after all – but he had wanted so badly to stay overnight in the Alamo. As the man had said, it would be the chance of a lifetime. A chance to live a moment in history.

"And we can accommodate one coach, too," added the organizer, "if you want to bring him along."

The man looked at Muck, who was now the one turning red. Travis knew what such an opportunity would mean to Muck. The Alamo was the reason Muck had agreed to this trip.

"Yay, Muck!" Fahd called out. "Do it!"

The others took up the call: "*Do it! Do it! Do it!*"

Muck looked helpless. He turned to Mr. Dillinger for guidance, and Mr. D's mustache danced with delight. "*Do it!*" Mr. Dillinger said.

"Kids?" Muck said, looking from Sarah to Travis to Nish.

"*Do it!*" they all said in unison.

Travis waited so he could walk out with Nish and Sarah. The three Screech Owls who would be camping out in the Alamo were carrying their equipment bags and talking excitedly about the night ahead when they passed by a small office and heard a familiar voice.

It was Jimmy Vim – and he was screaming at someone.

"That's bull!" the team manager was yelling. "You can't change the rules like they don't matter. Your own tournament promotion says 'Championship team will camp overnight in the Alamo.' It's right there in black and white."

Travis peeked in through the small window under the "Office" sign. Jimmy Vim was berating an official, who sat behind a desk. The manager had a brochure out and was pounding it with his finger.

"What's three more kids?" the organizer asked calmly. "There's room."

"They didn't win!" Jimmy Vim shouted. "And then you go and throw in their coach! What's *that* all about?"

"They're little kids," the man protested. "Their parents would expect them to be with a responsible adult they know and trust. Something happens, I don't want it coming back at me."

"Nothing's going to *happen*!" Jimmy Vim snarled. "It should be the Cheetahs alone in there tonight. Not some stupid arrangement you decide on at the spur of the moment."

The man shrugged. "Where's the harm?"

"The *harm* is you lied!" Jimmy Vim shouted, banging his fist on the brochure on the man's desk. "We won the tournament, we get the Alamo – simple as that!"

"Forget it," the man said, obviously tired of Jimmy Vim's rant. "It's a done deal. Live with it."

Jimmy Vim stood back and smirked. "Live with it," he repeated. "*Live* with it . . ."

Travis shuddered. He felt as if someone had just slid a large ice cube down the back of his shirt.

This guy gave him the creeps.

14

The Screech Owls were cleaning out the storage area they'd been given for their equipment. The Kansas City Cheetahs had already taken their stuff from their area next door and had left it a mess: empty Gatorade bottles, candy wrappers, tape balls, broken sticks, half-eaten sandwiches.

"Disgusting," Sam said as she looked in. "They better not treat the Alamo like this or they'll end up in prison."

Sarah went over and tore down the poster that had been on the wall, just as Data came rolling along to help.

"Let me see that," he said.

She unrolled the poster again so he could read the words.

I am the master of my fate;
I am the captain of my soul.

"Some inspiration," Sam snorted. "They're supposed to be a team, and this poster is all about achieving things by yourself. Makes no sense."

"I am the master of my fate," Data mumbled as he sped off in his wheelchair. "I am the captain of my soul. . . . I am the master of my fate; I am the captain of my soul. . . . I am the master of my fate; I am the captain of my soul."

"What's with Data?" Sam asked. "This isn't school – there's no memory assignments here."

Sam, Sarah, and Travis did a quick cleanup of the garbage left behind by the Cheetahs and then helped the rest of the Owls clean out their own area. They left it looking as if a professional cleaning crew had come through.

They were piling their equipment at the front doors of the arena when Data came spinning around the corner from the snack bar area, where Travis had earlier seen him set up with his computer. He seemed excited.

"*I found it!*" he shouted as he spun to a stop beside the rest of the team.

"Found what?" Fahd asked.

"I am the master of my fate," Data said with a touch of impatience. "I am the captain of my soul."

"And I am the tournament MVP!" Nish shouted, raising his treasured trophy above his head like it was the Stanley Cup.

"I did a Google search on it," Data continued, ignoring Nish and his trophy and looking down at his tablet. "I thought it might be from some song, but it's a poem."

"I hate poetry," Nish chimed in. Everyone ignored him.

Data referred to the website he had found: "The poet is English, William Ernest Henley,

1849–1903. He lost his left leg to tuberculosis and was the inspiration for Long John Silver in Robert Louis Stevenson's *Treasure Island.* Henley wrote a poem, 'Invictus,' about losing that leg and how he had to fight to recover. The poem is famous – it's where the line 'My head is bloody, but unbowed' comes from."

"What's that got to do with hockey?" Fahd asked.

"Sounds like me," Nish said. "My head was bloodied, remember?" No one paid him the slightest attention.

Data rolled his eyes. "It's *inspirational*, Fahd. Think about the last lines of the poem: 'I am the master of my fate; / I am the captain of my soul.'"

"I don't get it," Fahd said, shrugging.

"I know a poem," Nish chimed in.

Beans, beans, the musical fruit.
The more you eat, the more you toot.
The more you toot, the better you feel.
So eat your beans for every meal.

"*Can* it, idiot," Sarah snapped. She turned to Data. "But why would they choose a poem like that to fire them up?"

"Who says the team chose it?" Data asked. "Seems to me that this *team* is a one-man operation."

"No kidding," said Travis.

"There's one other thing," Data said, clicking the screen back to another website. He held it up so the others could see a picture of a sour-looking, sharp-faced man with a light-brown brush cut. He was dressed in orange prison overalls. Beside his picture was a story.

"Those two lines – 'I am the master of my fate; / I am the captain of my soul' – were the last words of Jaymes Voight before he was executed for the Kansas City bombing."

"*Who?*" said Sam.

"*What?*" said Jesse.

The Owls were now all gathered around Data as he read from the screen: "Jaymes Mitchem Voight, also known as the Kansas City Bomber, was executed on January 14, 2002, for blowing up a government building in Kansas City, Kansas, on May 30, 1996. He killed 78 adults and 9 children in what was considered at the time to be the worst terrorist attack on the United States. Voight spoke no final words before being executed by lethal injection but did leave behind a written statement quoting the poem 'Invictus,' by British poet William Ernest Henley. The poem ends with the lines 'I am the master of my fate; / I am the captain of my soul.'"

"Sick," said Sam.

"Bizarre," added Andy. "What a weird poem to choose."

"There's nothing wrong with the poem itself," said Data. "It's great – just a bit odd that it has this Kansas City connection. I wonder if the team even knows."

"Who cares?" said Nish. "This is getting boring. I wanna party!"

He hoisted his MVP trophy above his head again and walked around as if his teammates should be bowing at his feet.

"We're going to party," Sam said. "*You're* going 'camping,' remember?"

"Oh yeah," Nish said, looking crestfallen. "I forgot."

"Typical," said Sam. "He gets the chance to spend the night surrounded by history and he 'forgot.' Tell me, Mr. Nishikawa, do you ever think about anything but yourself?"

Nish feigned shock, batting his eyes quickly.

"Truthfully?" he said, then smiled. "No, I don't."

15

The entire team ate at a nice taco restaurant along River Walk and then most of the players headed back to their billets for their final night in San Antonio.

The Screech Owls who would be spending the night in the Alamo – Muck, Sarah, Nish, and Travis – were scheduled to show up at the front gate at dusk. It being a warm, clear night, they decided to walk the few short blocks to the historic fort rather than waste money on a taxi.

They were met at the front gate by the same U.S. National Park Service ranger who had given them the talk on the Alamo. Ranger Bill Norton was smiling and happy to see them.

"I guess you are my extra guests tonight," Ranger Norton said good-naturedly. "We have a little spare room. No showers, though." He laughed at his joke. "Still, it's a great privilege to be allowed to spend the night in the Alamo. You'll be in the barracks section, sleeping pretty much like the soldiers did a couple of hundred years ago. There are ghosts here, people say, so better we all stick together in one big room, right?"

"Sounds fine by us," Muck said.

The ranger showed them into their quarters. They had arrived before the Cheetahs hockey team, so had their choice of location. Travis, Sarah, and Nish wanted to be near the doorway – it was hot and muggy, and this might be one place where they would get a fresh breeze – and they went about getting set for the night with the sleeping bags and air mattresses the parks people had supplied.

After awhile, the big doors opened and Ranger Norton led in the Kansas City Cheetahs, each one carrying a small traveling bag. Jimmy Vim had a bag and also carried something else – a heavy box – placing it in a far corner and dropping his team jacket over it.

Butch Ruby and Muck hurried to greet each other like old friends, then introductions were made all around, Sarah, Nish, and Travis shaking hands with the various Cheetahs and exchanging names this time rather than congratulations. Travis was surprised to find Tanner Brady so friendly. The Cheetahs winger smiled when they shook hands and told Travis he had played well and deserved the all-star nod. Still, Travis couldn't shake his concern about the relationship between Tanner Brady and Jimmy Vim, who seemed to shake hands only with the greatest reluctance and could barely conceal his anger at having these intruders join the campout the Cheetahs had won.

Travis and Tanner Brady were talking near the corner where Jimmy Vim had set the box down. Several times Travis noticed Jimmy Vim watching them carefully, sneaking peeks whenever he thought Travis might not notice. But the Cheetahs' manager was too far away to hear their conversation over the general din of nearly thirty peewee hockey players getting ready to spend the night in the barracks.

"What was that box you guys brought in?" Travis asked.

"What do you mean?" said Tanner.

"The thing just there in the corner. Your manager put his jacket over it."

Travis pointed, hoping Jimmy Vim wouldn't notice. Tanner smiled. "Jimmy's always afraid someone's going to break into our bus, so he brought the skate sharpener in. He says it cost a lot of money."

"He never even used it," Travis said. "Our manager, Mr. Dillinger, had to sharpen your skates."

Tanner Brady seemed surprised. "Is that who did it? Best sharp I ever had."

"Mr. D's the best," Travis said, and let the conversation drift off to another topic.

Just then, the park ranger returned with a large basket. "Back in 1836," Ranger Norton told the group, "William Travis didn't have a cell phone, otherwise he could have called for extra troops. The soldiers didn't text message – they were way too busy with real life for such nonsense. So official Alamo policy, young gentlemen – and lady, sorry – is *no cell phones* for the night. I don't want you surfing or calling your buddies, and we certainly wouldn't want the world to see photos of your coaches in their pjs, now, would we?"

The players all laughed at the idea. "I'll collect your phones in a few minutes," Ranger Norton told them. "I'll give you enough time to let your parents know where you are and shut your phones down, okay? Be back in five minutes to collect them."

There was a flurry of activity as the peewee hockey players searched their pockets for cell phones. Travis didn't have to worry. He didn't have one. But he had called his parents earlier, and they knew exactly where he would be that night. They were excited for him.

Sarah did have a phone, and she was texting her parents when she noticed she had a message.

It was marked "Urgent." And it was from Data.

"What's this?" she said. Travis leaned over her shoulder to see.

"URGENT!" Data's message began. "I couldn't get it out of my head that 'Jimmy Vim' sounded like a fake name. So I did some anagram checking on the team you're with –"

"What's an anagram?" Travis asked before she could scroll down for more.

"Where they take the letters and scramble them to say something else," she said impatiently. "You know – like my name, Sarah, can also be 'a rash.'"

"No kidding," said Nish, giggling.

Travis shrugged while Sarah scrolled down. It seemed kind of silly to him. How could something called an *anagram* possibly be considered urgent?

Data's text message continued: "I took 'Cheetahs' and came up with nothing. But then I took the name of the Kansas City Bomber, Jaymes Mitchem Voight, and scrambled his name. The computer came up with 78,948 possibilities. One of them is 'Cheetahs got Jimmy Vim.'"

"Oh my God!" Sarah gasped.

Nish was also reading the message. "What's Data mean?" he asked.

"I don't know," Travis said. "It could be a coincidence, couldn't it?"

Sarah looked at him in disbelief. "You *think*?" she asked.

"I don't know what to think," Travis said.

But it was too late to get back to Data. The ranger was back in the room, collecting the cell phones. He was coming their way. Sarah had no choice. She shut off the cell phone and dropped it into the basket, where it was quickly covered up by dozens of other phones.

"What do we do now?" Travis asked.

"I don't know," Sarah said.

She shivered, though it was a hot and muggy night.

16

The kids played olden-days games: cards and board games rather than video games or mini-stick hockey, which was what they'd do if they were staying in a hotel. After a couple of hours, they all settled down for the night in the large, barren room. It was dark, but not pitch-black dark, as the whitewashed walls gave the place a ghostly glow. It made Travis shiver.

He couldn't sleep. Neither could Sarah.

"There's got to be a connection!" she whispered.

"But what?" Travis whispered back.

"Think about it," she continued quietly. "They have this poster up on the wall and Data tracks the poem back to this guy who blew up the building in Kansas City and killed all those people. Then Data unscrambles that guy's name and finds 'Jimmy Vim' and 'Cheetahs' in it. That creep's name never sounded right to me in the first place."

It hadn't sounded right to Travis, either. Or to Nish, who was now equally convinced there was something very odd about Jimmy Vim and his involvement with the Kansas City hockey team.

"What do we do?" Travis asked.

"Take Muck aside and tell him everything we know," Sarah said.

"He'll think we're *crazy*," protested Nish.

"But what if we're right?" Sarah asked. "What happens if we do nothing?"

Travis shivered. "I don't know. Let's talk to him."

Muck wasn't in the barracks. They found him just outside, strolling around the walls, stopping every so often to study another plaque describing the history of the Alamo.

"What's up?" Muck said with a smile when he saw them. Travis felt awful spoiling Muck's evening – he seemed perfectly happy lost in the events of 1836.

"Can we talk to you?" Sarah said.

Muck seemed surprised. "Shoot," he said.

They told him about the poem on the wall of the team's dressing room – "I am the master of my fate; / I am the captain of my soul" – and how Data said it was from a poem that this guy who'd killed all the people in Kansas City had quoted just before he was executed.

"It's a very famous poem," Muck said. "Lots of people quote it."

Then they told him about Data's work unscrambling the guy's name, how it could be rearranged to make the words "Cheetahs" and "Jimmy Vim."

Muck suddenly became very interested. "When did you learn this?" he asked.

"Just this evening," Sarah said. "Data sent me a text message before I handed over my cell phone."

Travis noticed Muck's right cheek moving in and out, as if he were clenching and unclenching his jaw. His voice was calm, but inside he seemed to be churning.

"Have you noticed anything here?" he asked.

"What do you mean?" asked Nish.

"Anything unusual?" Muck asked.

"Jimmy Vim brought his portable skate sharpener in," Travis said, practically giggling. "He was afraid to leave it on the team bus in case someone stole it."

"He can't even use it," added Sarah.

"Can't use what?" asked Muck.

"He had to get Mr. D to do his team's skates. We don't think he even knows how to use it."

Muck looked very concerned. "Where is it?" he asked.

"He put it down in a corner," Travis said. "And covered it with his jacket."

"Let's go have a look," Muck said.

The four of them turned and headed toward the barracks. They made their way discreetly down the far side of the room to the back corner.

There was a Cheetahs team jacket on the ground – but no portable skate sharpener.

It was gone.

17

"Nishikawa!" Muck spoke sharply. "Find the ranger! And hurry!"

Mumbling and muttering, not sure what was going on and without a clue where Ranger Norton might have gone to, red-faced Nish hurried off.

Muck was quick to action. "We have to find where he's gone with this," he said.

"What's wrong?" Sarah asked.

Muck sniffed. "We don't know what's in that

box. But I guarantee you, it doesn't hold any skate sharpener."

Travis looked around the barracks carefully. "Tanner Brady's gone, too," he said.

"The memorial," Muck suddenly said. "Let's go!"

Travis looked at Sarah. Why would Muck want to go to the big stone memorial dedicated to the defenders of the Alamo? Now wasn't the time to ask questions, however, and they instinctively followed their coach.

Muck was moving as quickly as his bad leg would let him. "You two be extremely careful!" he said over his shoulder. "If we find something, we do nothing until the rangers come."

But find *what*? What could Jimmy Vim and Tanner Brady possibly be up to? What could be in that box if it wasn't a skate sharpener?

There was no time to stop and discuss it. They hurried along the corridor leading from the barracks toward the courtyard of the Alamo, Muck leading the way and Travis and Sarah following quickly along behind.

Muck was first into the courtyard. Night was falling, and the only illumination was the glow of the city reflecting in the clouds overhead and a few security lights along the walls. It was not quite dark, but dark enough.

Muck suddenly stopped, holding up a hand like a warning to Travis and Sarah behind him. The two players stopped fast, too. Travis was breathing hard, but it wasn't because he was out of shape. He was scared – but scared of *what*?

Muck crouched down. Sarah and Travis crouched beside him. Across the dim courtyard they could see the tall, white memorial, but there appeared to be no one near the huge structure. Muck seemed to be looking just beyond it.

The two Owls followed their coach's gaze. There, in the dark, they could make out a figure deep in the shadows. Whoever it was, the person was crouched down by the old well where the defenders of the Alamo had once drawn water for themselves and their horses.

Muck squatted low and began to creep toward the figure. He didn't find it easy, given his bad leg.

But he moved cautiously, keeping low and quiet. He held his hand up by his shoulder to ensure Travis and Sarah stayed where they were. The last thing he wanted was for them to get hurt.

He could make out the figure tying a rope around something. It appeared to be a box. Could it be the box for the phony skate sharpener?

"*What do you think you're doing?*" a voice snarled somewhere off to the side.

Muck turned. He couldn't see the face. He didn't need to. He knew the voice of Jimmy Vim. It had a ratlike quality to it – grating and whiny.

"What do you think *you* are doing?" Muck asked as he straightened up.

"None of your damned business," Jimmy Vim answered.

Muck's eyes had adjusted to the dim light by now. He could see that the figure wrapping rope around the box was Tanner Brady. He had heard the exchange and was looking up, frightened.

Muck could now see that Jimmy Vim held a gun. It was leveled right at him. Muck knew he couldn't do as he wished – just walk over and give

Jimmy Vim, the sleazy creep, a great slap before the rangers arrested him.

He was also worried about the kids behind him. He wished they hadn't come. He knew he would have to cooperate with Jimmy Vim in order to protect the kids.

"Put your hands behind your back," Jimmy Vim demanded.

Muck did as he was told. He could feel Jimmy Vim behind him, then felt a patch of duct tape being slapped over his mouth. He couldn't call out to warn anyone. He then heard the duct tape ripping as Jimmy Vim used it to wrap around Muck's wrists. Muck now couldn't call, couldn't act. He had to hope that Nish had found the ranger and help was on its way.

"What do we do?" Sarah whispered to Travis, both of them still crouching in the shadows a fair distance away. They could see that Jimmy Vim was doing something to Muck's hands. They knew Muck would submit to that only if Jimmy Vim had a knife, or perhaps even a gun.

Travis swallowed hard. Here was his "line in the sand" moment. He, Travis Lindsay – nearly two centuries after William Travis had called upon his men to give everything they had for the Alamo – had to do something.

Travis didn't answer. He knew what he had to do.

He moved quickly, sticking to the shadows, staying close to the ground, but picking up speed.

He came in toward Jimmy Vim from behind, suddenly launching himself through the air like a missile, straight into the backs of Jimmy Vim's knees.

The man buckled, both the duct tape and the handgun he'd been holding flying through the air. Sarah was right behind Travis – linemates forever – and she kicked the gun as hard as she could so that it slid across the ground and vanished in deep shadow.

What do I do now? Travis wondered as he rolled on his back, dazed.

But events were out of his hands. He could hear shouts and see flashlights bobbing as others ran into the courtyard.

It was Nish – and right behind him were several rangers.

Nish, leading the cavalry to the rescue!

18

It seemed to take but a moment, and it seemed to take forever. Travis's mind was racing one instant, felt frozen the next. As the images piled up, he tried to make sense of all he was seeing and hearing.

Muck's hands had been freed, and he was rubbing his wrists where the duct tape had dug in. Sarah was showing the rangers where the handgun had spun out of sight. One ranger put on rubber gloves and picked up the gun and placed it carefully in a plastic bag. Jimmy Vim was in handcuffs, being led away under the glare of bright spotlights that had come on as the rangers and Nish rushed into the courtyard. Tanner Brady was standing off to the side, with a ranger on each side of him.

He was crying. No, he was bawling – great, huge sobs, rattling and shaking his body as he stood there, suddenly looking very small between the two rangers. Travis had a funny feeling. It struck him that Tanner Brady wasn't crying from being scared or from being caught. The star of the Kansas City Cheetahs was sobbing with relief.

The San Antonio police, accompanied by several FBI agents, came and took Jimmy Vim away. They also took Tanner Brady away, but not with Jimmy Vim. The Cheetahs manager was locked in the back of an armored police van, which drove off with lights flashing and siren blaring. Tanner Brady left in a police cruiser with a friendly policewoman sitting beside him in the back.

The Screech Owls all assembled together at the Alamo the next morning and Ranger Norton spoke to them to explain what had happened. A member of the San Antonio police force was there, too, as well as an FBI agent.

Jimmy Vim, to no one's surprise, was not Jimmy Vim at all. He had no identification on him, but his fingerprints showed he was in fact Terry Bartholomew, a twisted fanatic who idolized Jaymes Voight. Terry Bartholomew was seeking revenge for what the law had done to Voight. He had purchased an IED through a criminal network.

"That stands for Improvised Explosive Device," the FBI agent explained. "IEDs are homemade bombs. They were used to blow up tanks and kill soldiers in Iraq and Afghanistan."

"His idea was to blow up the Alamo," the FBI agent continued. "Whether he planned to set it off some night or during the day, when the courtyard was packed with tourists, we don't know. But the idea was to attack America right in the heart of its greatest sym-bol of freedom. Blow up the

Alamo and the message to the rest of the world would be pretty frightening."

"What about Butch?" Muck asked.

"Butch?" asked the FBI agent.

"Butch Ruby, the coach of the Kansas City team. He's a friend of mine."

The police officer took this question. "Your friend is in rough shape, sir," he said. "Mr. Ruby is blaming himself for having had anything to do with this character. He says this man calling himself Jimmy Vim came along and offered enough money to purchase a bus and equip the team for the year. All he asked in return was to be taken on as manager. Mr. Ruby says he was personally against it, but he was outvoted by the parents. They wanted to be 'big league,' and the coach says he couldn't do anything to stop it."

Muck shrugged and shook his head. Travis couldn't imagine him ever agreeing to such a thing – nor could he imagine the Screech Owls' parents being so blindly greedy.

"What part did Tanner Brady play?" Travis asked.

"We're still working on that one," said the policeman. "From what we gather, it was also about money. Jimmy Vim had promised Tanner Brady's family ten thousand dollars if they let him move to Kansas City and play for the Cheetahs. If the team won the San Antonio Peewee Invitational tournament, the family would get an additional ten thousand. Tanner Brady's mother is not well, and his father is out of work. Money is a powerful persuader. The Brady family is just sick over this – they had no idea what this Jimmy Vim character was up to. The plan was to lower the kid down into the well during the night so that the IED could be hidden. Jimmy Vim couldn't do it alone, and he needed someone smaller than himself to get down there, someone light enough that he could lower and raise him by rope. We think he planned to detonate the explosive on a day when the Alamo was filled with tourists."

"What will happen to Jimmy Vim now?" Sarah asked. "Or Bartholomew or whatever his real name is?"

"He will appear in court this afternoon and be

officially charged with conspiracy to commit a terrorist act against the United States. He will be given a fair trial, but I wouldn't think we'll ever hear from Mr. Vim, or Mr. Bartholomew, again. As for Tanner Brady, he should be free to go home to his family very soon. The kid was plainly forced to cooperate with Mr. Vim, so he's not going to be in any trouble with the law."

"What about me?" a voice squeaked from a back row.

The three officers craned their necks to see who had spoken. The Owls all turned as one, staring hard at the beet-red face of Nish, who was getting to his feet.

"I'm sorry . . . ?" the FBI agent asked, confused.

Ranger Norton leaned over. "That's the young man who got the rangers to the scene in time."

"Oh," the FBI agent nodded, smiling. "The United States of America is most grateful for your help, young sir."

"Do I get a medal?"

The three police stared. The Owls stared. Sarah and Sam shook their heads in bewilderment at the nerve. Muck shut his eyes and pretended he wasn't hearing what he just heard.

"Well?" Nish asked, looking around as if expecting everyone to remember that he was the hero of this adventure, peewee hockey superstar, tournament MVP, who had just saved the Alamo.

No one answered his question. No one could.

19

The Screech Owls were on their way home. They had said good-bye to their billets. Nish, Sarah, Travis, and Muck had all been interviewed by the San Antonio media – "that's *N-I-S-H-I-K-A-W-A*" Nish spelled out to every one of them. And Ranger Bill Norton had come to the airport to see them off and give them all special U.S. National Park Service badges. Nish thought he should still get a medal to go with his MVP trophy.

When a slight delay was announced for the Owls' flight to Chicago, Muck asked Mr. Dillinger if he'd join him in a coffee, but Mr. D, lost in his crossword puzzle, just shook his head no.

Muck picked up his drink at a small kiosk away from the gate where the Screech Owls were waiting to board their flight. He paid the man at the cash for his steaming cup of coffee and made his way over to the stand where the cream and sugar were set out. He put two creams into his cup and looked around for something to stir it with. There being nothing in sight, he returned to the cash.

"Stirrer?" Muck asked.

"Right beside the sugar," the man answered, barely glancing up.

"Nothing there," Muck told him.

This time, the man looked to see for himself.

"I could have sworn . . . ," he said. "Sorry about that." And he hurried around the counter with a fresh box of stirrers to put beside the cream.

"Not to worry," Muck said, and plucked out one of the tiny plastic straws and stirred his drink before placing a lid on it for the walk back to the boarding gate.

When the coach of the Screech Owls got back, he found his entire team surrounding a red-faced Nish, who seemed deep in an argument with Sam and Sarah.

"I did 155!" Nish was protesting. "The Guinness record is 151 – so I broke it by four!

Sam pointed down to a great pile of what appeared to be tiny brown plastic sticks that looked like they'd been thrown – or *spat* – onto the floor.

"Those aren't straws," Sam said, shaking her head. "They're *stirrers.*"

"They're *straws*, too!" Nish protested. "Look."

He picked up one of the straws, put it to his mouth, and sucked hard enough that the others could hear air whistling through.

"No way," Sarah said. "They're stirrers."

"Tiny straws!" Nish whined.

"Stirrers," Sarah repeated.

"Stirrers," Travis agreed.

"Stirrers," said Sam.

"*Stirrers!*" shouted about a dozen of the Owls at once.

Nish looked like he would burst. He looked like all the air he had just sucked in through that tiny stirrer was exploding inside of him.

"Maybe you set a new world record for stuffing coffee stirrers in your mouth," Sarah suggested with a wicked smile.

"STRAWS!" Nish tried one last time.

Muck stepped in. "More like a record for *stealing* coffee stirrers," the coach said in his quiet voice. "Come with me, Mr. MVP World Record Holder – there's a man in a small coffee shop down the way who would like to meet you."

Nish looked at his coach's face, then at his coach's hand, where a cup of fresh coffee was steaming.

He swallowed hard, his face turning crimson.

"And," Muck added with a stern look, "it isn't to get your autograph."

CHECK OUT THE OTHER BOOKS
IN THE SCREECH OWLS SERIES!

MYSTERY AT LAKE PLACID

Travis Lindsay, his best friend, Nish, and all their pals on the Screech Owls hockey team are on their way to New York for an international peewee tournament. As the team makes its way to Lake Placid, excitement builds with the prospect of playing on an Olympic rink, in a huge arena, scouts in the stands!

But as soon as they arrive things start to go wrong. Their star center, Sarah, plays badly. Travis gets knocked down in the street. And someone starts tampering with the equipment. Who is trying to sabotage the Screech Owls? And can Travis and the others stop the destruction before the final game?

THE NIGHT THEY STOLE THE STANLEY CUP

Someone is out to steal the Stanley Cup – and only the Screech Owls stand between the thieves and their prize!

Travis, Nish, and the rest of the Screech Owls have come to Toronto for the biggest hockey tournament of their lives – only to find themselves in the biggest *mess* of their lives. First, Nish sprains his ankle falling down the stairs at the CN Tower. Later, key members of the team get caught shoplifting. And during a tour of the Hockey Hall of Fame, Travis overhears two men plotting to snatch the priceless Stanley Cup and hold it for ransom!

Can the Screech Owls do anything to save the most revered trophy in the country? And can they rise to the challenge on the ice and play their best hockey ever?

THE GHOST OF THE STANLEY CUP

The Screech Owls have come to Ottawa to play in the Little Stanley Cup Peewee Tournament. This relaxed summer event honors Lord Stanley himself – the man who donated the Stanley Cup to hockey – and gives young players a chance to see the wonders of Canada's capital city, travel into the wilds of Algonquin Park, and even go river rafting.

Their manager, Mr. Dillinger, is also taking them to visit some of the region's famous ghosts: the ghost of a dead prime minister; the ghost of a man hanged for murder; the ghost of the famous painter Tom Thomson. At first the Owls think this is Mr. Dillinger's best idea ever, until Travis and his friends begin to suspect that one of these ghosts could be real.

Who is this phantom? Why has he come to haunt the Screech Owls? And what is his connection to the mysterious young stranger who offers to coach the team?

SUDDEN DEATH IN NEW YORK CITY

Nish has done some crazy things – but nothing to match this! At midnight on New Year's Eve, he plans to "moon" the entire world.

The Screech Owls are in New York City for the Big Apple International Peewee Tournament. Not only will they play hockey in Madison Square Garden, home of the New York Rangers, but on New Year's Eve they'll be going to Times Square for the live broadcast of the countdown to midnight. It will be shown on a giant TV screen and beamed around the world by a satellite. Data and Fahd soon discover that, with just a laptop and video camera, they can interrupt the broadcast – and Nish will be able to pull off the most outrageous stunt ever.

Just hours before midnight, the Screech Owls learn that terrorists plan to disrupt the New Year's celebration. What will Nish do now? And what will happen at the biggest party in history?

PERIL AT THE WORLD'S BIGGEST HOCKEY TOURNAMENT

The Screech Owls have convinced their coach, Muck, to let them play in the Bell Capital Cup in Ottawa, even though it means spending New Year's away from their families. It's a chance to skate on the same ice rink where Wayne Gretzky played his last game in Canada, and where NHLers like Daniel Alfredsson, Sidney Crosby, and Mario Lemieux have played.

During the tournament, political leaders from around the world are meeting in Ottawa. To pay tribute to the young hockey players, the prime minister has invited the leaders to watch the final game on New Year's Day. The Owls can barely contain their excitement!

Meanwhile, as Nish is nursing an injured knee off-ice, he may have finally found a way to get into the *Guinness World Records*. But what no one knows is that a diabolical terrorist also has plans to make it a memorable – and deadly – game.

SCREECH OWLS

Photo credit: Fred Lum / *The Globe and Mail*

ROY MACGREGOR was named a media inductee to the Hockey Hall of Fame in 2012, when he was given the Elmer Ferguson Award for excellence in hockey journalism. He has been involved in hockey all his life, from playing all-star hockey in Huntsville, Ontario, against the likes of Bobby Orr from nearby Parry Sound, to coaching, and he is still playing old-timers hockey in Ottawa, where he lives with his wife Ellen. They have four grown children.

Roy is the author of several classics in hockey literature. *Home Team: Fathers, Sons and Hockey* was shortlisted for the Governor General's Award for Literature. *Home Game* (written with Ken Dryden) was a bestseller, as were *Road Games: A Year in the Life of the NHL*, *The Seven A.M. Practice*, and his latest, *Wayne Gretzky's Ghost: And Other Tales from a Lifetime in Hockey*. He wrote *Mystery at Lake Placid*, the first book in the bestselling, internationally successful Screech Owls series in 1995. In 2005, Roy was named an Officer of the Order of Canada.